THE FLAW IN
ALL MAGIC

BEN S. DOBSON

For Abby and James, who remind me constantly of the power of imagination (and who are way too young right now to actually read this book).

PROLOGUE

───────

SOMEONE WAS IN the room with her.

Allaea Hesliar was digging through the endless shelves of the artifice workshop for an uninscribed copper sheet when she heard the footsteps. No one else should have been there. It was after midnight, and she was working long past her scheduled hours.

"Indree? Is that you?" Of course it was. Who else would it have been? Indree's constable badge got her past the workshop wards, and lately she'd decided that Allaea was putting too many hours into the airship project. *Come to drag me into the fresh air again, no doubt.* "I'm back here."

No answer, but the footsteps started in her direction. The funny thing was, they weren't coming from the entrance, but from further inside. Had Indree come in and headed for the worktables at the back without Allaea hearing? Unusual—elven ears didn't miss much. But then, she *had* been absorbed in her work.

Allaea sighed. The last thing she needed just then was Indree's mothering. The heating glyphs for the airship's envelope were still less efficient than she liked, and final inscription had to be done tomorrow in preparation for the launch, only two days away. She'd already submitted her spell diagram for the evening deadline, but a better solution had come to her that night as she'd lain awake in bed. If she could have it done by morning, she could still get Dean Brassforge to approve the change. All that was left was to test a working mock-up. What she *really* needed was a damned copper plate, and they were never where they were supposed to be.

"You don't have to keep checking on me, Indree." She extracted herself from the shelves, stowed several components in the pockets of her topcoat, and went to meet the approaching footsteps. "You're my dearest friend, and I love you, so please don't take this the wrong way, but you're an insufferable nag and I wish we'd never met."

It wasn't Indree.

Allaea turned the corner to see a man in dark clothes standing before her in the shadowy aisle between shelves. His face was covered by a dark cowl with holes for eyes, like an executioner's mask.

She let out a startled yelp and backed away a step. "Who in the Astra are you? This place is off-limits. How did you get in?" There were privileged projects being worked on in the University's primary artifice workshop, the airship chief among them. No one got by the wards without a properly glyphed badge.

"You weren't supposed to be here," was all the man said. At least, all he said in Audish. He raised a hand, and started to mutter a spell in the *lingua magica*.

Allaea spoke the quickest barrier spell she could muster. A sheet of silver-blue energy shimmered into existence in front of her just as the man completed his own spell. Silver flame crashed towards her in a wave that broke against her shield.

Spellfire. He was throwing spellfire. If it touched her, it would melt the flesh from her bones in an instant. *He's actually trying to* kill *me.*

She couldn't hold her hasty shield much longer under that kind of assault. It was already failing.

Allaea turned, and ran.

"Help!" she shouted, for the guards or for Indree—and she wished more than anything that Indree *had* come, now. She would have known what to do. She was a constable, trained in combat magic. Allaea knew ancryst machines inside and out, but she'd been lucky to get that shield up at all, and any other spell that might help seemed to have deserted her. "Help me! There's someone in here!"

She raced down aisles of shelves, darting through whatever gap brought her closer to the exit. Her legs ached, and she was moving too fast for the tight corners—she had to yank herself around by the edges of the shelves, dislodging gems and components. A trail of fallen artifice pieces littered the floor behind her.

She could hear him following, quick footsteps against the stone floor. He was chanting in the *lingua* again, readying a spell to burn her alive. From somewhere deep in the workshop behind came a distant howling, with an icy crackle behind it that sent a chill through her blood. *What in the Astra was that?* She didn't want to find out.

Her lungs burned and her breath came in short, terrified gasps, but she was nearly at the door. Just around the next corner, and then…

She put her foot down wrong; her ankle turned, and she stumbled sidelong against a shelf. She put her hand out to catch herself, and knocked over a collection of iron rods and copper plates—*there* they were.

No, no, no. She had to keep moving, couldn't afford this. Panicked, she risked a look over her shoulder.

He rounded the corner behind her, still chanting. Lifted his hand.

Allaea screamed as silver flame roared over her skin and dissolved her sight.

CHAPTER ONE

——

TANE CARVER KNEW something was wrong the moment the clock began to chime.

It was the students. There weren't enough of them. Normally the clock atop Thalen's Hall tolling the hour would have sent hundreds of young humans and elves and gnomes and more scurrying to their classes, but today the campus was nearly empty. A few dozen students scattered about, and that was all.

The University Guard were out in force, though, patrolling the cobbled paths in their silver-on-blue uniforms. Two stood at the entrance to every building, new and old—from the functional brick of the artifice workshops to the ancient stonework of the cathedral-like invocation hall. At every door, guards were stopping what few students approached, making them display laurel wreath badges to identify themselves. Tane hadn't been back since he'd been expelled two years prior, but unless the University of Thaless had become a prison camp since then, he had to classify that as unusual.

He felt the familiar high-altitude pressure in his ears that always preceded a sending, and then a voice spoke in his head. *"Mister Carver, I'm reading you on campus. Don't dawdle. I'm waiting."* Liana Greymond, Dean of Divination. Tane had come at her request, though he'd considered refusing—he didn't much want to hear a lecture on how badly he'd embarrassed the University. Ultimately though, he'd been curious enough to chance it. After two years, she wouldn't have contacted him without reason.

"*I know you're eager to see me, but try to contain yourself, Dean Greymond,*" Tane answered without speaking—through her spell, not his own. She'd left the link open, an Astral channel that he had no way to replicate. "*You'll make me blush.*"

A slight pop in his ears as the pressure abated, and Greymond's presence was gone. He'd been her favorite student once, but even then she'd never had much patience for his sense of humor.

Tane studied what few students he saw as he walked—without hurrying—toward the divination hall. They mirrored the population of the Audland Protectorate at large, half of them human like him, and half a diverse selection of the magical races: a dwarf here, an elf there, a doll-sized sprite fluttering down the path beside a nine-foot tall ogren. All wore the silver-on-blue laurel wreath badge of the University displayed proudly at the breast of their topcoats. And they all looked so *young*, though he was only a few years older now than they were.

Most kept their heads down and walked quickly, avoiding eye-contact, but a small group had gathered on the open grass at the campus center, whispering in hushed tones. Tane didn't need divination to sense their unease. As he watched, a dwarven man in University Guard uniform approached the little congregation and hurried them on their way with a few words. They moved on without argument.

What is going on? Tane regretted not asking Dean Greymond while he'd had the chance, but she wouldn't have answered in any case, not until he was sitting in front of her.

He was still watching the little group disperse when someone bumped into him.

"I'm sorry!" A squeaky voice from somewhere near his waist. "I wasn't watching—Tane?"

Tane looked down to see a dark-skinned gnomish woman with a broad face and large eyes, her hair arranged in a rather severe bun. For a moment, she flickered before him, her skin and clothes taking on the greens and greys of the grass and cobblestones behind her—the natural gnomish ability to mask themselves with illusion when they didn't want to be seen.

"Roona," he greeted her. "Just when I was beginning to worry they'd replaced everyone I used to know with children." He'd shared classes with Roona Nackle, though she'd concentrated in invocation and he—ostensibly, at least—in divination. She would have advanced to graduate studies by now. An opportunity he'd never gotten. "You must know what all this is about. If the guards were wearing different colors I'd think the campus had been occupied by an invading army."

"I... I'm not sure exactly. Something happened last night, but everyone's heard a different story. I haven't..." Roona trailed off and looked rather unsubtly over her shoulder, then fumbled her pocket watch from her waistcoat and gave it a cursory glance. "Listen, Tane, I have to—"

"Stop talking to me before someone sees you?"

She had the grace to look sheepish, at least. "I'm sorry. It isn't personal, it's just that... people still talk about you, you know, and I'm on the list for a faculty position next year."

"I understand." Tane forced a smile. "The price of infamy. It's fine. Go."

Roona went, a little bit more eagerly than he would have liked. It was hard *not* to take that personally.

The divination hall was at the far eastern end of the campus, but it didn't take him long to cover the rest of the distance. The oppressive mood in the air was making him nervous, not to mention curious, and either one was enough to overpower his admittedly petty desire to make Dean Greymond wait.

A three-story marble building topped with a brass-domed observatory, the divination hall cast a long shadow across the grass in the pre-noon sun. Outside the main doors, two of the University Guard stood watch: a dark-bearded human man and a stout dwarven woman. Each of them wore a shortsword and a single-shot ancryst pistol at the waist, and a laurel wreath University badge at the breast—though theirs would have different glyphs on the back than the students, allowing them to pass through more secure wards.

"Badge?" the dwarf asked, eyeing Tane's frayed waistcoat and rumpled shirt with suspicion.

"Don't have one," said Tane. "I'm Tane Carver. Dean Greymond asked me to come."

The human nodded. "Carver, right." There might have been a flicker of disapproval in the man's eye, but he didn't let it enter his voice. "She left word. Go on in. Straight to her office, please." They pushed open the doors and held them until Tane had passed.

Inside, the building was lit with globes of magelight hanging from the ceiling, glowing in the familiar silver-blue common to all Astral energy. Tane passed only a few students—for the most part, he heard nothing but the echo of his own footsteps against marble floors.

Greymond's office was on the third floor just below the observatory, and the hall leading up to it was empty, save for two guards outside a small study room. One was a short brown-scaled kobold, watching Tane with slitted reptilian eyes, but it was the larger woman who drew his attention—grey-skinned, muscular, easily six and a half feet tall. *An orc?* They weren't entirely unheard of on the Audland Isle, but orcs were rare outside their homeland of Sverna at the far north of the Continent. He'd never seen one on campus—they had no affinity for magic whatsoever.

But no, her features weren't quite right for an orc, either. She had the size, the greyish skin, the glinting yellow eyes and pointed ears, but her flat nose and protruding jaw weren't as pronounced as they might have been, and she lacked the short tusks sticking up from her lower lip. Grey-white hair that was almost like fur framed her face, but the similar fur on the back of her hands and arms wasn't near heavy enough, and while her fingernails were dark and thick, they were no orcish claws. She had to be a half-orc—almost unheard of in the Protectorate, or anywhere else.

The woman caught him staring and grinned, exposing sharp lupine teeth. Embarrassed, Tane looked away, and walked faster. He heard her chuckling behind him as he moved down the hall.

It wasn't far to Dean Greymond's door. When he raised his hand to knock, it swung open before his knuckles touched wood, leaving him rapping on air.

"Tane Carver. It has been a long time. Come in." Liana Greymond was a human woman of a young-looking fifty years, her face only slightly lined beneath short dark hair. She sat behind a desk cluttered with papers, a silver-blue magelight lamp standing at one corner. She didn't appear to be looking at Tane, but rather somewhere *through* him. Those faraway eyes were customary for her, as if she was seeing things no one else could.

She usually was.

"I hate when you do that," said Tane. "Let me—"

"Do something before I respond to it?" Greymond finished. "Why waste the time?" That was a habit of hers. Sometimes she caught glimpses of things a half-second before they happened, and Tane was convinced she enjoyed using that foresight to put people off balance. "Please, take a seat." She muttered a spell under her breath in the *lingua magica* and gestured to a chair in front of her desk. It pulled out for him to sit as if drawn by an invisible hand.

Tane sat, shifting uncomfortably under her appraising eyes. He was suddenly all too aware of what she was seeing:

an unkempt, unshaven man of average height and build with untidy brown hair and shabby clothes. His appearance didn't say much for the life he'd been living since his expulsion, working odd jobs—and not always entirely legal ones—wherever he could peddle his education in magical matters. He hadn't cared with Roona or the guards, but Liana Greymond had been something of a mentor to him once. He ran two fingers along the watch chain attached to his waistcoat, and then dipped them into his pocket to rub the dented brass watch casing there—a habit, when he was uneasy. It didn't tick beneath his fingers. There hadn't been clockwork inside for a long time.

"I assume this is about… whatever it is making everyone so nervous out there," he said by way of distraction. "If you're looking for a good scapegoat, I'll take the fall, but know that my price isn't going to be cheap."

"This isn't a laughing matter, Mister Carver," Greymond said. "I understand you are working as a consultant of sorts, now. On magical matters, proofing spell diagrams and the like. Is that correct?"

That was a generous way of putting it, but Tane wasn't about to argue. "You must—"

"Yes, of course I looked into it before I summoned you. I was simply confirming. You aren't misrepresenting yourself to anyone as a graduate mage, I hope?" She was peering through him again, a slight furrow of concentration at the corners of her eyes.

"Are you casting a truth-spell? I'm insulted, Dean Greymond." Tane smiled innocently. "When have your divinations ever caught me in a lie?"

Greymond let out a short, sardonic laugh. "I suppose that's true. Four years as my best student without an ounce of magic to your name, and I never guessed. You know how to evade a divination, I'll grant you that. But please, humor me."

"I haven't misrepresented anything," said Tane, and by the look on her face, it passed muster with her divination.

It *was* the truth, this time. "That's the point. I'm *trying* to show people that you don't need to be a mage to understand magic." *It's usually better if you aren't,* he thought but didn't say.

"Yes, I recall the nature of your final dissertation. That's why I asked you here, in fact. I wish to acquire your services. I'm loathe to say it, but the University has need of your... rather peculiar area of expertise."

"In other words, you need me to find a loophole in a spell that your mages can't." Tane leaned forward, intrigued. "This *is* about whatever happened last night, isn't it?"

Greymond frowned, her eyes glazing for a brief instant as she searched the Astra for some answer or another, and then she nodded. "What I am about to tell you is not to be shared until the chancellor makes it public. Do you swear to abide by that?"

"I suppose I have to, don't I?" said Tane, and he meant it—at least for now. Anything else would have triggered her truth-spell. "I'm not about to leave here without knowing now that you've made it so mysterious. And you know I can keep a secret."

Greymond was silent for a moment—confirming his sincerity with her divinations again, or perhaps just weighing the decision. But she *would* tell him. She wouldn't have asked him here otherwise. He expected it would be a poorly formulated spell for an artifice project or the like, something the University administration needed fixed quickly and quietly. Perhaps something for the airship in drydock at the waterfront—it was meant to launch the day after next, the first ancryst-powered flying machine, and they wouldn't want word of any problems getting out now.

But what Greymond said next wasn't what he expected at all.

"A student was killed on campus last night, Mister Carver."

CHAPTER TWO

———

"WHAT?" TANE SHOOK his head. *I can't have heard that right.* "Are you telling me someone was *murdered?*"

"I am," Greymond confirmed.

"And you sent for *me?* Why not bring in the blue-caps?"

"Stooketon Yard is being notified, of course, but the chancellor wants to have this situation well in hand before we bring in the constabulary. The University's reputation must be considered, after all. To that end, there is a matter I believe you can help with. Let me explain."

"Please," said Tane. *A murder, and they need me for some reason. This could be the chance I've been waiting for.* It felt ghoulish to be excited about it, but helping here could get him a foot in the door with the University administration. They might actually *listen* to him this time.

"Shortly after midnight last night, someone accessed the primary artifice workshop. There were guards in the building, but they saw no one in the halls at any point. A... a student"—Greymond's eyes flicked away from his there, for an instant—"was using the workshop, considerably past the hours she was scheduled to be there. She was involved in the airship project, but those spell diagrams had already been submitted and approved. Still, she may have hoped to fit in some last-minute change before the final inscription of the glyphs this morning. The guards heard her screaming, but by the time they arrived, she was dead. Spellfire burns all across her face and chest."

Tane winced. "That's awful." Spellfire burned hotter than molten metal. The only thing worse was the fire of a true dragon—at least according to records from before the fall of the Estian Empire, when such creatures still lived.

"It was... difficult to look at," Greymond said, and by the look on her face, she was seeing it again now. She didn't say anything for a moment, and then, "Nothing was stolen from the workshop, so we must assume murder was the intent. The building was quickly closed, and a second student was apprehended, hiding in the graduate workshop down the hall. Our only suspect, but a likely one. He was seen arguing with the victim earlier that day. He claims he was meeting someone in the building, but he won't provide a name, and my divinations say he is lying."

"Sounds like—"

"If the matter was already solved, Mister Carver, I would not have sent for you. Will you let me finish?"

Tane almost laughed at that. *When has she ever let anyone finish?* But he leaned back in his seat and motioned for her to continue.

"The issue is this: our suspect should not have been able to enter the primary workshop at all, and certainly not without triggering an alarm. The wards and detection spells on that room should only allow University staff, faculty, and students with properly glyphed badges—those involved with the rather privileged spellwork being done within. And the constabulary, of course." All campus wards had an exemption for the bluecaps, in case of emergency. "As I said, the victim was one of Dean Brassforge's apprentices, assisting with the airship project. The suspect had no such access, nor did we find a stolen badge anywhere on him. We've accounted for all of the badges with access among faculty, students, and guard. None seem to be missing."

There it was. The reason she'd asked him here. Wards could be restricted in near limitless ways: by specific name or title or physical feature, by badge or passphrase, by any number of arbitrary criteria or simply by the caster's whim. But they all shared the same ultimate purpose, which was to keep people out. When they didn't, it was almost always because of careless magecraft.

And finding careless magecraft was Tane's specialty. "You want me to see if I can find a flaw that might have let him in."

"Precisely," said Greymond. "Either he found a way to exploit our wards, or someone else with access sneaked by the guards. We need to know which, at the very least. The wards have been recalibrated to allow only constables, high-level faculty, and University Guard for the time being. With the airship so close to completion… Lady Abena has invested a great deal into the project, and we cannot afford a lapse in security only days before the launch ceremony. Chancellor Nieris is eager to resolve the matter before then. He has charged me with overseeing the investigation."

Hoping she can divine an answer before they have bluecaps crawling over the campus, no doubt. Tane understood the stakes now. It was common knowledge that the Protector of the Realm had put much of her political capital into the airship project. She'd given·a number of speeches in the Senate of Houses to that effect, touting the age of peace and prosperity that would result from improved trade and travel between the Audland Protectorate and the nations of continental Calene—relations that had been strained since the Mage War had dissolved the Estian Empire into squabbling factions centuries ago. And the University couldn't afford to displease the Lady Protector if they wanted to maintain their operating budget.

If Tane proved himself useful here, it could change everything. *It might get me out of double-checking the glyphs on fenced artifacts just to pay rent, at least.*

But there was something else. Greymond wasn't using names, and the way she'd avoided his eyes for a moment there... "Wait," he said. "This woman, the victim—if she was on the airship project, or any project in that room, for that matter, she must be a graduate student." Which meant she might have been a classmate of his. And one name came to mind above all others, one woman who would easily have qualified for such a prestigious apprenticeship. *Not her. Please.* "Do I... did I know her?"

Greymond sighed, and Tane's heart fell into his feet. "I should have known it wouldn't take you long. I'm afraid so."

No. He clutched the arms of his chair, and waited.

"I'm sorry, Tane. It was Allaea Hesliar."

A wave of relief swept over him, and he felt awful for it. Allaea had been a friend, once—an elven woman with a sharp tongue and a passion for ancryst machines. She deserved better. *But it's not Indree.*

And then the full weight of it hit him. Memories of long nights spent studying, the three of them trading notes and ideas and stupid inside jokes. Allaea had been kind, and clever, and never shy about letting him know he was being an ass—and now she was dead. Burned alive in the worst way imaginable. He hadn't seen her for two years, but it hurt, even so. *Spellfire, Indree must be devastated.* He'd only known Allaea *through* her, and those two had been inseparable friends long before he'd met them. He swallowed against the lump rising in his throat. "Does Ree know?"

"I can't say. Miss Lovial took her considerable talents elsewhere after graduation. But if this is too difficult for you..."

"No. I want to help." He didn't imagine Allaea had thought very highly of him after the way he'd left the

University—or the way he'd left things with Indree—but he owed her this much.

"I hoped you would." Greymond shuffled through the papers on her desk and slid several towards him. "These are the diagrams for the wards on the workshop, and the detection spells. I... when I learned who she was, I thought of you, and that dissertation of yours. You always were the best at finding the cracks in whatever spell I put in front of you."

Tane flipped the spell diagrams around to face him and looked them over. Glyphs detailing the exact nature of the spell, directions for placement. A few things stood out to him as worth checking into, but they might have been incidental. There were always flaws and oversights. Casting a spell meant making a request of the Astra, the plane of magical energy that stood behind the physical world. And that energy always did exactly what it was told, for better or worse. A misused word or careless sentence structure could have disastrous effect. It was very much like all the old stories of magical wish-granting spirits—if there was the slightest way for the spirit to misinterpret the wish, it always did.

That was the essence of the dissertation he'd been expelled for: how dangerous spells could be when cast carelessly, especially when so many in the Protectorate relied on artifacts and machines created by mages. How even the non-magically gifted should be allowed to enroll at the University to learn how the magic they relied upon worked, how to check it for errors. How it was ludicrous to expect reliability from a spell that had only ever been proofed by the caster. And the centerpiece of the essay had been the fact that Tane had spent near four years as a student of magic at the University without any magic of his own, outsmarting every detection spell and excelling above the true mages in most of his classes.

The revelation had not been well received. Not even by the professor he'd most hoped would support him.

That still rankled, more than a bit. "If I was the best, why—"

"You think I should have stood up for you with the chancellor? After what you did?" Greymond narrowed her eyes, and a suggestion of anger heated her careful, professional tone. "Never mind how much you humiliated the University, did you ever think for a moment how humiliating it was for *me*? The Dean of Divination fooled for *four years* by her favorite student? If you'd just come to me with the truth at any point, I might have…" She stopped herself, took a long breath. "It doesn't matter now. We aren't going to do this. Just look at the spells."

She's right. Don't ruin this chance. "It's going to take longer than a few minutes to study these," said Tane. "I'll have to bring them back to my office." By which he meant the narrow brick-front single room he rented in Porthaven by the docks.

"Not the originals. I will have copies sent to your address."

"Fine. 17 Tilford Street, in Porthaven. I'll also need—"

"No. Under no circumstances may you enter the workshop. We can't have anyone interfering with evidence before the constabulary investigates, and your involvement is not something I want widely known. The spells were cast from those diagrams, and I promise you they match perfectly. That should be enough."

Disappointing, but Tane had expected that. "Fine. Then I need to know a few things. You've checked the glyphs for wear?" Magic always needed specific instruction. Without a mage's active concentration, long term spells used engraved glyphs of the *lingua magica* to direct their energy.

"Of course. They were redrawn last month, and have been double and triple checked against the diagrams. A perfect match, as I said."

"No sign of Astral tampering?" Tracing a spell's Astral link and deconstructing it was extremely difficult for even the most skilled diviners, and it took a great deal of time and effort, but it was possible.

"None. It would have set off a number of detections."

"Were the gems replaced recently?" All spells needed a source of Astral energy. Absent a mage, most used gems or crystals charged in advance, linked to the spell glyphs with magically conductive copper. That was the other, slower way to beat a ward—simply waiting for the power to fail.

"A week ago, and plenty of energy left in them. We hardly need you to point out the obvious, Mister Carver."

"And your divinations? Did you find anything I should know?"

"Very little, sadly. I was able to witness Miss Hesliar's final moments through the Astra, but they didn't offer a great deal of guidance."

"Show me."

Greymond frowned. "Are you sure? It isn't a pleasant memory, and I know you were close."

He wasn't sure at all, but if there was any chance that he might see something she hadn't… "Do it."

Greymond's eyes focused somewhere behind his head, and pressure built in his ears for a moment before the sending came to him, halfway between a memory and a waking dream.

For some reason he'd expected to see Allaea, but instead he was looking through her eyes, at an aisle of shelves stacked with artifice tools and materials. The workshop. She was moving quickly, running from something. He could hear her breath, heavy and frightened. There were footsteps behind her, and a male voice, chanting in the *lingua magica*. She stumbled, put out a hand, knocked several bits of metal from a shelf. Until then there had been a part of Tane that didn't believe it, but he knew her by that hand—long, delicate elven fingers callused and scarred from tinkering with ancryst machines. She looked over her shoulder, caught a brief, blurred glimpse of a dark figure rounding the corner, wearing a masked cowl like an executioner's hood. The figure reached out toward her.

Allaea screamed as her vision dissolved into silver flame.

Tane's ears popped as the sending faded. He took a shaky breath, and tried to focus on the facts instead of the pain in that scream. "Not... not much there, with the mask." That was unfortunate but not uncommon—when a diviner could call up the last memories of the dead, smart murderers covered their faces.

"As I said."

"What about this suspect the guards found, then? He'd know better than anyone how he beat the wards. *If* he did. You say your spell caught him in a lie, but that could mean a lot of things. You know as well as anyone that truth-spells aren't perfect. They can be misled." Tane himself was living proof of that. All a truth-spell did was reach through the Astra to read a subject's mental and emotional state, both of which could be controlled. Or the opposite—agitation could make true statements look false to a spell. "If he'd really planned to kill someone, I'd expect him to have invented a better story."

"A fair point," said Greymond. "But added to the rest of it, the lie certainly doesn't speak to his innocence."

"Who is he? Anyone I know?"

"The same year as you, but beyond that, I'm not sure. Kivit Thrung."

"I've met him." A goblin student, concentrating in artifice like Allaea. He'd always been over-competitive in class. Goblins weren't exactly highly respected as mages—he'd always had to prove he deserved to be there. Tane knew how that felt. "Things can change in two years, but... he always seemed too nervous to hurt anyone. Could—"

"Yes, I thought you might want to talk to him." Greymond answered the unasked question with a nod. "That I can arrange. He is just across the hall—I was

questioning him before you arrived. As I said, my divinations caught him in a lie, but he refuses to explain further.
Given your history, you might get something out of him
that I couldn't."

"As a fellow liar, you mean?" Tane said, quirking an
eyebrow.

"Essentially, yes. You mimicked divination in my
class for years—in the absence of magic, I must assume
you did so by reading behavior. That may prove useful.
Come." Greymond stood, and led him out of the office.

Across the hall and a short distance down, the two
guards Tane had passed on the way were still standing at
attention. Greymond approached them.

"Let us in," she said, and the half-orc woman pushed
open the door, held it, and followed them in. Her partner
remained outside to watch the hall.

Inside, a scrawny goblin man with grey-green skin sat
hunched over the table, the tip of his long nose pressed
flat against the wood. A pair of round spectacles sat low
on his face, threatening to fall off at any moment. He
didn't look up. "I already told you I didn't do it!" he said in
a high, nasally voice.

Tane glanced at Dean Greymond, who gave him a
slight shake of her head—she was still detecting a lie. They
sat down across from Thrung while the half-orc guard
took her place in front of the door.

"Ask what you will," Greymond said.

Thrung finally raised his head then, and saw Tane. He
pushed up his spectacles, and small black eyes narrowed
beneath the lenses. Thick goblin eyebrows knit together to
form a single line of bushy black hair. "Carver?" He
looked to Greymond. "What is he doing here?"

"Helping," Tane said quickly. "Can I ask you a few
things?"

Greymond, for once, didn't interrupt—she just sat silently, watching Thrung sweat. Apparently she was willing
to let Tane take the lead on this.

Thrung's eyes moved wildly from side to side. "I already told them, I was just meeting someone. I swear!"

It was impossibly obvious that he was lying, divination or no. The real question was what about. By necessity, Tane had learned how to read people fairly well, and this didn't strike him as the manner of someone who had just burned a rival alive. "Calm down, Kivit. I want to help, if you'll let me."

Hope brightened Thrung's face immediately. Predictable—a drowning man would cling to whatever happened to float by. "You understand what it's like, don't you, Carver? To have everyone distrust you? They just think I did it because I'm a goblin."

"And, to be fair, because you were the only one in the building, and you were seen arguing with Allaea earlier." Hope was important, but he couldn't let Thrung forget the stakes, either.

"I didn't kill her!"

Tane held up a hand. "Of course you didn't." He really did want to believe that, but if it was a lie, he meant to find out. For Allaea's sake. "But it would help to know what you were arguing about."

"She took my spot on the airship project! My diagrams for the heating glyphs in the envelope were far more elegant, and we both knew it. But a goblin was never going to be picked over an elf. I just wanted her to admit it, that's all. I promise I didn't want her dead."

Tane could see why Greymond thought Thrung had done it. He wasn't exactly helping himself. "And you were meeting someone in the artifice workshops that night? Who?"

"Just... just a girl. I don't know her name. A... a friend thought we might enjoy each other's company, and set it up."

"Really? You couldn't come up with anything better than a nameless girl in the artifice workshops at midnight?" Tane leaned forward over the table. "You and I both know

that isn't going to beat Dean Greymond's divinations."
Someone else might have, but it would have taken a great
deal of self-control, and Thrung clearly wasn't very much in
control of anything just then. "Let me tell you what they
already believe, Kivit: that you were jealous of Allaea for
taking your spot, so you waited in the workshops until late
at night, snuck in, and burned her alive with spellfire.
They're *already* at that point, so when you're caught in an
obvious lie, it only makes you look worse."

Thrung's cheeks went an ashy shade of grey. He really
was easy to lead. "I would *never*... I couldn't... my badge
doesn't even have *access* to that workshop!"

"Exactly," said Tane. "So whatever the truth is, it
must be better than what they think. Just tell me, and we
can get you out of here."

"I... They won't believe it. It... it sounds bad."

"It can't sound any worse, I promise you."

Thrung's shoulders slumped. "I suppose you're right.
I... look, you have to understand I wasn't going to hurt
her. I just wanted her to admit my designs were better. I
was... I was waiting for her, that's true. I was watching the
door from the workshop down the hall. I meant to confront her when she left. Then I heard the scream, and the
guards came, and... I panicked. I hid. And when they
found me, I lied. If I'd admitted I was there for her...
People always want to believe the worst of a goblin. But
that's the truth, I swear it."

Again, Tane glanced at Greymond.

"That reads as true," she said. "You would have
saved us a great deal of time if you'd said so earlier, Mister
Thrung."

Thrung just hung his head. "I'm sorry, Dean Greymond. I just—"

"Wait," said Tane. "You were watching the door the
whole time? You must have seen the real killer go in."

"That's the thing," said Thrung. "That's why I didn't
say anything. It... it doesn't sound very good for me."

"What do you mean, Mister Thrung?" Dean Greymond was staring slightly past Thrung now, with that faraway look that said she was concentrating on the Astra, not the physical world.

Thrung swallowed, his long neck convulsing nervously. "What I mean is that I watched that door all night. *No one* went in."

CHAPTER THREE

"YOU *HAVE* TO let me look at the workshop!"

"Absolutely not," said Dean Greymond. They were standing in the hall just outside the room where they'd questioned Kivit Thrung.

"If he didn't do it, and no one went in or out, it raises a thousand questions," said Tane. "Even if someone had been waiting inside since before Kivit got there, how did they get out after the building was closed down? No illusion would have done it once the guards were on alert." True invisibility was impossible—the closest thing was the instinctive gnomish ability to blend into their surroundings with illusion, which was extremely difficult for a mage to emulate consciously. And it didn't hold up well under scrutiny. "That leaves, what... a portal? That's dangerous magic." An improperly stabilized portal could swallow whoever stepped through it into the Astra—not to mention the things that could come *out*.

"You know we have very strict portal wards," Greymond said. "Only the deans or the chancellor can make a portal into or out of University grounds, and it wasn't one of us—we had a meeting in Chancellor Nieris' office that night that went very late, and no one was absent."

"That's exactly my point," said Tane. "This looks impossible at a glance. Whoever did it might have left some sign, and just looking at diagrams isn't going to tell me—"

"It's all you're going to get, Mister Carver. You did well with Thrung, but I shouldn't have let you go that far. I have to admit, I was... curious. To see what you could do, now that I know you have no magic. But the constabulary will be arriving soon, and we can't have you running around the University where someone might get the wrong idea. Can you imagine how it would look if word reached the Gazette that you were assisting in the investigation?"

"Dean Greymond, please." Tane needed this. His friend was dead, and he needed to know who had done it, and why—and beyond that, solving an impossible crime where the mages of the University and Stooketon Yard couldn't would go a long way towards proving the point he'd been trying to prove for years. "I just want to help."

"And you can. It will help us a great deal to have those diagrams proofed for errors, and you will be paid well for it. That is your role here. Nothing else."

She isn't going to listen. I'm wasting my breath. Tane nodded. "Of course, Dean Greymond. I'm sorry, I'm just... invested in this. Allaea was my friend."

Greymond's eyes narrowed and took on that faraway look. Looking for lies. "Mister Carver, promise me you won't try to get into the workshop."

Careful. Easy breaths. "I won't."

She watched him a moment longer, pursed her lips, drummed a finger against her leg. Finally, she turned to the guards at the door. "You," she said to the half-orc. "Escort Mister Carver off campus. See that he goes nowhere but out through the gates."

"Yes," the half-orc woman said, and took Tane's arm in a startlingly firm grip. "Come." She had a strong Svernan accent—the Audish words came out short and clipped.

Tane went along without a fuss. It didn't matter. He'd already made his choice, and Greymond's divinations had been easy enough to evade.

He was getting into that workshop, one way or another.

Outside, on the front steps of the divination hall, the half-orc released his arm. "Don't run," she said in her heavy accent. "I am faster." She bared her teeth in a wide, unsettling grin.

"I don't doubt it," Tane said agreeably, matching step with her down the path toward the campus center. He was going to have to slip her guard before they reached the gates, or he'd never get back in, but for that he'd need to put her at ease first. "Forgive me if this is nosy, but you must come from Sverna by your accent. We don't see very many orcs here who weren't born on the Isle." The orcish homeland was highly isolationist, and they had no magic there—quite the opposite of the Protectorate. But then, Svernan orcs weren't supposed to approve of breeding with humans either, and here this woman was. "It feels like there's a story there, if you don't mind telling it?"

"Clever man," she said with another toothy grin. "I was born in Sverna, yes. There, do what clan chief says, every day. Everything is… ordinary. Boring. I wanted to see things. See magic."

"Well you came to the right place," said Tane. "There's nowhere more magical than the Protectorate, and most of it is here in Thaless." He stopped, and extended his hand. "I'm Tane. Carver."

She squeezed his hand too tight and shook vigorously. "Kadka, of Clan Nadivek. Or was. Now not so much."

"It's a pleasure, Kadka. Have you been here for very long?"

"Only month, little more," she said. "Is still new for me." That was good. She might not know the best paths across campus yet. "But not new for you, yes? Sivisk"— that must have been the kobold guard—"tells me you were student in magic here with no magic. How do you fool so many mages for so long?"

"Trickery and deceit, mostly," Tane said. "I'm strong at magical theory, which made the practical parts easy to fake."

"Teachers never ask you to make spell?"

"Of course, but that's not so hard. A little sleight of hand—" He reached behind Kadka's ear and produced a brass coin, to her obvious surprise, then flipped it into the air, caught it, and spun it across his knuckles. "—and you'd be surprised what you can do. An artifact up the sleeve to duplicate one spell or another, that sort of thing. With proper misdirection, they never notice a thing." She was still staring at the coin in his right hand when he opened the left one, revealing the silver-on-blue enameled badge he'd plucked from her coat.

She laughed, a too-loud cackle of delight. "You *are* clever man. But why do they never make spell to catch lies, or see if magic is yours?"

"Those can be fooled, but no one is casting them in the first place if they don't have reason to. I didn't give them a reason. It's like this: there are three schools of magic a student can concentrate in. Invocation and Artifice both require harnessing magical energy with showy words or glyphs, and you're expected to produce tangible, physical results. Divination is all about quietly searching the Astra for answers that you can usually get out of people without any magic at all, and if you get one wrong, well, it's known to be an unreliable art. I'll give you one guess where I declared my concentration."

"So you are like mage with no magic," said Kadka with an impressed nod. "You must know much about spells, to do this for so long. This is why Greymond asks for your help?"

They were nearing the narrow gap between the lecture theatre and Thalen's Hall—the administrative center of the University. There were no guards in sight. And Kadka seemed charmed by his story, for the moment.

He wasn't going to get a better chance.

"Something like that," Tane said. "And I *want* to help. The woman who died… I knew her."

Kadka frowned. "I am sorry. There is no good way to lose friend, but that is bad one."

"That's why I wanted a closer look. I know you're supposed to bring me to the gates, but maybe we could stop by the artifice workshops? We don't have to go in, I just… I want to see for myself that they're taking the investigation seriously."

She hesitated. "Greymond says—"

"I know. Look, though." He still had her badge in his hand, and he flipped it over to show the polished brass on the back where the glyphs were engraved. On this side, glinting in the light, it looked like nothing more than a strangely patterned coin. "These glyphs are keyed to the campus wards. They determine who can go in and out. Without one of these, I can't get anywhere I'm not supposed to, so…" His foot caught on a cobblestone, and a glinting circle fell from his hand, rolling away into the grass. "Well that was stupid. Can you see it?"

Kadka stepped off the path, kneeling to look for her badge.

The moment her back was turned, Tane bolted.

He darted into the narrow alley between buildings just ahead and to his right. Kadka shouted what might have been a Svernan curse—"*Deshka*," it sounded like—and then he heard her running. He took a left into the alley behind the dining hall, where a locked gate barred the way. With any luck, Kadka would see that and assume he'd gone the other way, which would cost her time heading back toward the lecture theatre before joining with the main footpath on the other side.

But Tane had cut through this gate many times when he'd been a student. The latch was easy to flip.

He rounded the next corner and froze, holding his breath and waiting for the patter of Kadka's feet passing by the little alley. And there it was—she was going the wrong way. *Thank the Astra.*

Tane exited the alley onto the open grass of the campus center. From there it was a quick sprint across to the artifice workshops on the north side.

He was panting as he neared the broad brick building, but he couldn't see Kadka behind him yet. He forced himself to slow down and breathe through his nose. *Don't want to look too suspicious to the guards.*

There were two men at the door, a broad-shouldered human and a dwarf with thick mutton-chop sideburns. *Spellfire, let them not recognize me.*

"Gentlemen." Tane gave them a nod, and strode confidently for the door.

The dwarf moved to block his way. "The building is closed, sir."

Tane flashed them Kadka's badge—he'd palmed it up his sleeve and dropped the coin for her to chase. "That's why I'm here," he said. "Dean Greymond asked me to double check the wards, make sure no one has access who shouldn't. We don't want the scene tampered with before the constables get here." He shook his head sadly. "That poor girl. I hope they catch the bastard who did this soon." Greymond had said they were still keeping the murder quiet—just knowing about it would make his story credible.

"Damn right," said the big human. "No one should die like that." He waved his partner aside. "Go on in. It's the one at the far end of the hall."

Tane pushed through the doors, risking a quick glance over his shoulder. Still no sign of Kadka, but she wouldn't be long. It would take her a moment to explain why she didn't have her badge, and then they'd come after him.

He didn't have much time.

Two smaller workshops sat at either side of the mage-lit hall, but Tane hurried toward the far end. The primary workshop took up most of the back half of the building, an ample space for artificers to develop the magical devices and machines that made their small island nation a powerful force in the economy of the Continent.

The door wasn't locked. Tane was certain that the keys to most doors on campus had been misplaced long ago out of simple disuse—the wards were meant to be an improvement over any mundane lock.

But they hadn't been enough to protect Allaea.

I hope this works. If it didn't, it was going to be like walking into a wall. He took a deep breath, and stepped forward through the open doorway. He felt a familiar tingle on his skin, and the hair on the backs of his arms stood up as he met the wards.

And then he was through.

There was no time for relief. The guards would be coming soon.

The workshop stretched open before him, a vast, warehouse-like space stacked with shelf after shelf of artifacts and components and ancryst machines in various states of disassembly. The metals common to artifice glittered in the dim magelight: copper for conductivity, brass for insulation, silver for amplification, gold for stability. Stacks of tubes and plates were interspersed with brass chests, carefully sealed to protect the magically reactive ancryst stone within. Gears and cogs and rods of iron and steel were strewn everywhere—Astrally inactive metals that wouldn't interfere with the magic fields that drove ancryst machinery. High up on the walls, in the shadows near the ceiling, he could vaguely make out glyphs of the wards surrounding the room.

And there was the body.

Tane hadn't seen her at first. She'd been left for the bluecaps to examine with their divinations, lying face-down on the floor some ten feet back, half-hidden between shelves. Devastatingly close to the door. *If she'd just been a little bit faster…*

He knelt beside her. Her head lay on its side, staring back at him with scorched, empty eye-sockets. *Thank the Astra Indree isn't here to see her like this.* He wouldn't even have known it *was* Allaea if Greymond hadn't told him. Much of her skin had melted and sloughed from her skull, leaving exposed patches of blackened bone crumbling to powder in places. Only a few locks of blonde hair remained on her scalp, clinging to patches of flesh the spellfire hadn't touched. Tane's stomach lurched, and he had to look away.

I'll help find whoever did this to you, Allaea. I promise you that.

There were no scorch-marks anywhere but on her flesh, no signs of fire behind her. Despite its great heat, spellfire went only where it was aimed by a mage, and burned only what it was permitted to burn—assuming, of course, that the spell was worded properly. But scattered metal parts and stray gemstones marked the way she'd come, knocked from the shelves in her haste. The trail led deeper into the workshop. There was something strange about that. *If he snuck up on her with the intent to kill, how did she get this far? He should have been between her and the door, but it looks like he was chasing her this way.*

A sudden thud came from the doorway, and a grunt of pain. Tane leapt to his feet and looked toward the sound.

Kadka was outside, rubbing her nose where it had struck the wards. She gave him a rueful grin. "Forgot. No badge."

She was, as far as he could tell, alone. "Where are the other guards?"

"Outside. I tell them I have message for you from Dean Greymond."

"What? Why?"

Kadka shrugged. "Tell them you stole badge, maybe trouble for me. We leave quietly now, maybe not."

"You're not angry?" Orcs had a reputation for ill temper, though Tane supposed that could easily be rumor and prejudice. There weren't many of them in the Protectorate to judge by.

"Why be angry? You wanted to help friend. And chase is more exciting than standing by door all day." She grinned again, and then cocked her head. "How are you inside? Even with badge, should only let in deans and guard now, yes?"

Tane's fists clenched with an anger he knew all too well. He forced one open, found the brass watch casing in his pocket, and touched the familiar dents and scrapes. "I'll tell you how. Someone was careless. There are two wards on this room. The first is used in secure areas all across campus, a general purpose ward that keeps out anyone but registered faculty, staff, and students. Present *and* former students, so they can bring wealthy alumni through when they need donations. The second ward narrows access to anyone who can get through the first and has a properly glyphed badge. When they restricted the wards, they didn't change the first one, and I *am* in the registry as a former student. Expelled, but that's a kind of former. That phrasing was the first thing I noticed when Greymond showed me the ward diagrams. They did restrict the badges allowed through the second ward, but University Guard badges still have access." He flashed her badge. "And I have this.

"Small oversights. Easy to correct. But nobody did, so here I am. They assumed no one would get by both wards, or maybe no one noticed the problem at all—no mage is going to look very closely at some glyphs in the corner once the spell's been cast. Any of the staff who maintain those glyphs and the gems that power them might have caught it, but they don't know what they're looking for. Menial jobs like that are *beneath* a trained mage. People who can't cast spells don't *get* to understand them.

"You came here for the magic? Well, let me tell you the most important thing about magic, Kadka. There's a flaw in all of it, the same flaw in every spell: the mage. When they make a mistake, who's going to challenge them on it? *That's* why I'm standing here. That's why my friend is dead. Because there's always—"

A distant howl cut off the end of Tane's diatribe, something like an animal's call with the low crack and groan of sudden frost behind it. It had to have come from deeper in the workshop, but it sounded somehow further away than the size of the room would allow. His heart thumped against his chest, and he half-turned toward the sound, then back toward Kadka.

She was staring past him, a focused glint in her eye. Drawing her shortsword with one hand, she beckoned to Tane with the other. "My badge," she said in a low voice. "Something is in there with you."

CHAPTER FOUR

————

TANE TOSSED KADKA her badge. She caught it in her outstretched hand and stepped freely through the wards.

"Stay," she whispered, and started down an aisle between shelves, toward the source of the sound. She moved with the easy, silent grace of a predator—a wolf stalking prey.

Tane hesitated a moment, and then followed. Kadka just shrugged, and held a finger to her lips.

The noise had come from the back end of the shop, past the shelves, where the artificers' worktables stood cluttered with parts and spell diagrams. At the last row of shelves, Kadka halted Tane with a raised hand and peeked around the corner, then beckoned him closer. Tane crept toward her and stole a look.

Between the worktables, a shimmering silver-edged hole in reality split the air. Through it, Tane could see another room, but it was hard to discern any details—the image rippled and distorted, like he was seeing it through a translucent silver-blue curtain shifting in the wind. It could have been anywhere.

"What is this?" Kadka asked, barely loud enough to hear.

"A portal," Tane breathed. "That's not supposed to be possible." He'd never even *seen* an open portal before—he'd been taught the theory, but opening tears in the world through the Astra was the most dangerous kind of magic, and his teachers hadn't dared demonstrate. The strict portal wards on campus shouldn't have allowed anyone but the heads of the University to open one here. Tane had only ever heard of it being done once in recent memory, when an ancient sub-basement of the invocation hall had collapsed over a decade ago, and even then only after every other way of freeing the trapped students had been tried.

The sound came again, a distant, icy howl. *Is that the portal? Are they supposed to make that noise?* He'd read of portals making strange sounds, but he didn't have the experience to be certain.

And a tear in the Astra doing *anything* unexpected was a very bad sign.

He was still watching the portal when Kadka tapped him on the shoulder. She gestured past the silver-blue rift, toward the back of the workshop where a bank of drawers ran along the wall—storage for spell diagrams. A figure in black was bent over one of the drawers. By size and build, he was probably a human or half-elf. From behind, Tane couldn't tell what he was doing, and a dark cowl hid his face.

Exactly like the cowl Allaea had seen in her last moments.

"Have to stop him," Kadka whispered. "This time, you stay." With a slight grin, she stepped around the corner.

She made no sound as she stalked across the floor toward the intruder. Tane watched, holding his breath, expecting the man to turn around with each step she took. But he didn't, and she was closing the distance rapidly.

This has to be the man who killed Allaea. The portal explains how he got by the guards, but why come back? Tane inched around the corner, straining for a better look. He had no intention of following Kadka—he couldn't move any-where near as quietly—but if he could just get a glimpse of the drawer the man was looking at...

The tip of Tane's foot slid beyond the front edge of the shelf.

Instantly, the intruder spun on his heel. His cowl cov-ered his face, but his head swiveled toward Tane's position among the shelves as if guided there by magic.

He must have had a detection spell up! But Kadka... And then Tane remembered: orcs were said to have a very weak Astral presence. He'd read of divinations struggling to detect them at all. *Damn it! She would have had him if I'd just stayed still!*

It was only then that the intruder noticed Kadka, not twenty feet away from him. He uttered a muffled curse under his mask. There was something in his hand, but Tane couldn't tell what it was before the man tucked it away behind his back.

For a moment, neither Kadka nor the intruder moved. Both glanced toward the open portal—about halfway between them and several yards to the left, from Tane's vantage point.

And then the man lunged into motion, sprinting for the rift at desperate speed.

Kadka was faster by far. She vaulted onto a nearby table, leapt across the next, and landed on her feet between the portal and the man in black. He skidded to a stop, spun, and ran for the shelves.

He can't get away. That was the only thought going through Tane's head as his feet carried him into the open. He leapt in front of the intruder, and they collided with jarring force. Tane fell back, and the other man landed hard on top of him, knocking the air from his lungs.

The man in black was on his feet in an instant. Kadka was already coming for him, her sword drawn. Tane heard the man utter a short spell in the *lingua magica*, and tried to warn her, but he couldn't get his breath.

Silver-blue force rippled from the black-clad mage in all directions—a precisely targeted spell would have taken too long to recite, with Kadka closing fast. A crushing pressure shoved Tane along the floor into a nearby shelf, and hurled Kadka against the worktable behind her. She grunted in pain as the edge of the table hit the small of her back.

The man bolted for the portal, half turned, and sent another wave of force crashing over them. Kadka ducked beneath one of the tables, gripping the anchored leg to weather the spell; Tane couldn't get on his feet in time to take cover. Silver magic pressed him hard against the shelf behind him.

Unmoored by the spell, the shelf swayed dangerously, and started to topple.

Tane tried to scramble out of the way on his hands and knees. Heavy metal and gemstones clattered to the floor on all sides. The shadow of the falling shelf stretched across the floor in front of him.

He wasn't going to make it.

A grey hand tufted with white fur gripped him by the wrist, and yanked him forward. The shelf struck the ground just behind him with a thunderous crash; on either side, several others swayed and fell just as loudly.

Kadka pulled him to his feet.

"Thank you," Tane gasped, but she was already whirling to chase the intruder.

The mage was nearly at the portal now. Kadka drew the brass-barrelled ancryst pistol from her belt and took aim. *Spellfire, no.* All ancryst machinery was based on one property—that the translucent green stone reacted to the presence of magic by moving in the opposite direction, the way lodestones repelled one another from the wrong ends. When she pulled the trigger, the firing charm would be consumed in a burst of magical energy, propelling a lead ball with an ancryst core from the barrel of the weapon.

Toward a portal into the Astra—the very essence of all magic.

"Kadka, wait!" Tane shouted, already running toward her.

He was too late. She pulled the trigger, and the pistol discharged with a silver-blue flash.

Tane tackled Kadka to the ground as the ball ricocheted directly back from the portal. Splinters flew as it struck the table behind them, digging a long groove through the wood.

When Tane looked up, the intruder was already through the portal. On the far side of that silvery curtain, the man extended his hand to touch something Tane couldn't make out. The portal bulged at the edges, twisting and writhing.

Kadka leapt to her feet and hurled herself forward.

The portal snapped closed in a blinding burst of silver.

The man was gone.

"*Deshka!*" Kadka cursed at empty space, and then turned to Tane. "Are you hurt?"

"I've been better, but no permanent damage," said Tane.

"Captain will not like this. Let you steal badge, let this *poska* go." She gestured vaguely at where the portal had been.

"He didn't get away entirely clean," said Tane. "I took this when he ran into me. He tried to hide it when he saw us." He reached behind his back and pulled a brass cylinder from his belt. It looked like a scroll case, capped at one end.

Kadka laughed. "Clever man with clever hands. This is important?" She peered at the tube as she stowed her sword and pistol.

Tane was about to answer when the lights began to flicker. Directly above, one of the magelight fixtures in the ceiling blinked out. Suddenly, the already dim workshop was a great deal dimmer.

"Oh no. No no no." Tane looked over Kadka's shoulder.

There, in the exact place the portal had been, a hazy figure drifted a foot above the floor, glowing a faint silver-blue. Another light flickered out overhead, and the shape became more defined, easier to see. It was humanoid but lacked any sort of detail, just an outline of Astral energy with two points of intense lightning-blue for eyes.

A wraith.

Kadka turned to see what he was looking at, and her hand went back to her sword.

"Don't," said Tane, tucking the scroll case back into his belt and backing away from the hazy figure. "You can't hurt it that way." It was beginning to move towards them now, drifting slowly, still gaining its bearings in the physical world.

"What is it?" She copied his movement, backing away a step as the wraith drifted closer.

"A wraith. An Astral spirit." Some said wraiths were what remained of those lost in unstable portals, forced to wander the Astra until they found a way out. Others claimed that they were spirits of corrupted Astral energy, created by grievous abuses of magic. Tane didn't know *what* they were, just that they were extremely dangerous. "Whoever that man was, he had to close his portal without proper precautions to keep us from following him. He must have destabilized it. That's why portal spells are so restricted—make any mistakes, and these things get out."

"Dangerous?"

"Very. They feast on Astral energy, and the link to the Astra is everything that makes us who we are, mage or no. What people called the soul, before they knew what it was. You won't die without it, but... The Astra-riven aren't themselves anymore. Just shells."

Abruptly, the wraith blurred forward, moving toward Kadka with unsettling speed. The worktables did nothing to slow it—its silvery form passed through them as if they weren't there. It made no sound as it moved.

"Watch out!" Tane shouted.

Kadka leapt aside; the wraith passed silently by.

And kept moving toward Tane.

That wasn't right. Wraiths were drawn to Astral energy, and she should have been the nearest source. *Spellfire, her Astral signature is too weak! Just like with the detection spell!*

It had never been moving toward her—she'd just been standing between it and a much tastier meal.

Tane turned on his heel and ran.

Artifice debris was scattered all across the floor from fallen shelves—maybe some with enough magical charge to distract the wraith a moment, if he was lucky. As he moved he searched frantically through the mess for what he needed. *I know I saw... there!* Sticking up from between the slats of a fallen shelf was the brass casing of an ancryst engine, large enough that Tane could almost have fit inside if he curled into a ball. Brass was always used for an engine's outer shell, as an insulator—it stopped Astral energy from passing through, so no external magical force could disrupt the movement of the ancryst pistons.

Tane hopped over the broken shelves that stood in his way and knelt beside the engine, then risked a look behind him. The wraith approached erratically, drifting for short stretches to drain this small artifact or that, and then advancing in blurs of sudden speed. As it moved, the magelights overhead flickered and failed.

Just behind him, Kadka vaulted through the remains of the shelf to grab his shoulder. "This is not time for playing with machine! Run!"

Tane tugged at the engine casing's hatch, a twelve-inch square plate that provided access to the internal workings. It wouldn't open—it must have been bent in the fall. "We can't leave that thing free. They're only visible in the dark. If it gets out onto campus in the daylight..."

Kadka didn't hesitate, just gave a firm nod. "What, then?"

The wraith surged forward, and Tane threw himself out of the way just in time to avoid its touch. "It doesn't seem to want you! I'll keep its attention, just get that hatch open!"

She yanked it open in a single pull. "What now?"

"Give me a minute!" Tane scrambled back as the wraith moved implacably toward him. Something rolled under his foot. He stumbled, and barely caught himself on the edge of a fallen shelf.

The wraith loomed over him. Hazy fingers reached out, grazed his chest. A terrible cold radiated through his body. He sagged back against the ground, felt his awareness fading...

"Carver!"

Kadka's voice pierced the fog, and Tane rolled desperately to the side, gasping. *If it touches me again, I'm done.* And it was still there above him, a ghost made of silver-blue light. An indistinct hand grasped for his heart.

Beneath his foot, Tane saw what it was he'd tripped on: a copper rod some four feet long. *Just what I was looking for.*

He snatched the rod up, ducked beneath the wraith's reaching hand, and made for Kadka and the engine. "Get ready to close the hatch, when I say!" Rod in hand, he turned to face the wraith.

It was just behind him, moving fast.

Tane jammed one end of the rod into the hatch, braced it so that it pointed at the wraith, and let go. The wraith surged forward, crossing the last few feet almost faster than he could see.

And impaled a body made of magic on a rod of magically conductive copper.

The wraith dissolved into silver-blue mist, drawn along the length of the rod, and pooled inside the brass engine casing. It only took an instant. With his sleeve over his hand, Tane grabbed the rod and pulled it free. Even that short moment of contact through the cloth of his shirt was enough to send cold racing up his arm to the elbow.

"Now!"

Kadka slammed the hatch closed.

For a moment, they were both silent, watching the engine hatch. Nothing. No sign of movement. The seal was good, and the wraith was a creature of magic—it couldn't pass through brass.

Finally, Kadka looked up at him, grinning her sharp-toothed grin. "Is like this every day for you, or just lucky today?"

"Oh, it's all the time." Tane couldn't help but grin back. "That's the third one I've trapped since breakfast."

Kadka cackled and clapped him on the shoulder, and then they were both laughing, out of giddy relief as much as anything.

"You two seem to be having fun. I hope we aren't in-terrupting." A woman's voice, from somewhere amid the shelves nearer the door. Tane instinctively slipped the brass scroll case from his belt and let it fall in with the scattered artifice parts littering the floor—just another piece of debris.

In the space of a moment, a half-dozen constables of various races surrounded Tane and Kadka. All of them wore blue uniforms and distinctive brimmed caps, batons on one hip and ancryst pistols on the other. Constable's badges glinted at their breasts—gold shields with the Protectorate's gryphon at the center. Most were men—three humans, an elf, a kobold—but standing head and shoulders above the others was a nine-foot tall ogren woman, striking and statuesque, as her people always were. Even if Tane had been so inclined, trying to flee would be pointless. No one joined the constabulary without some skill at magecraft, particularly spells to locate and subdue suspects quickly and efficiently.

Behind them came another woman in the same uni-form, but with the gold cord of a constable inspector at her shoulder. She held her cap clasped under one arm. It was too dim to see her face very well, but she was half-elven, with slightly pointed ears and a build somewhere between human and elf, solid but lean. "Search them," she said.

The ogren bluecap grabbed Tane and Kadka and lifted them to their feet. The constables patted both of them down, taking Kadka's sword and pistol—and several knives she'd apparently had hidden on her. Tane raised an eyebrow after the third; she just grinned back at him.

"Nothing stolen, Inspector," the elven bluecap said when he'd finally confiscated all of Kadka's blades.

When the ogren woman released his arm, Tane let himself fall, feigning a loss of balance. He landed hard on his ass, and winced. "Ouch." A quick grab behind his back and he had the scroll case again. He tucked it surreptitiously into his belt and pulled his waistcoat down to hide it.

"Get him up," said the half-elf, and the ogren did just that, hauling Tane roughly to his feet.

The half-elf approached, near enough that Tane could see her clearly even in the weak light. Her skin was a tawny brown, and her black hair was pinned up so that it would fit under her constable's cap. Her face was more elven than human, long and delicately featured with high cheekbones. When she reached Tane, amber eyes that he would have known anywhere widened in sudden recognition. "Tane?"

"Indree?"

CHAPTER FIVE

———

THE OGREN BLUECAP had to duck her head to enter the waiting room outside the chancellor's office, escorting Tane and Kadka in behind Indree.

"You can go, Laertha," said Indree. "See that no one else enters the workshops without permission. I don't want the scene contaminated any more than it already is." She threw Tane an annoyed glance, there.

The ogren woman nodded. "Understood, Inspector," she said in a perfect, melodious voice, and then ducked back out the doors.

Tane rubbed his arm where the big hand had gripped it—rather more tightly than he liked. "Is all this really necessary, Ree? You know we aren't criminals."

"Constable Inspector Lovial," Indree corrected. She didn't bother to respond to the rest of it. "My friends call me Ree. We aren't friends."

"Constable Inspector?" Tane said. "Already? Always the over-achiever." He hadn't expected to see her in a bluecap's uniform, but it was no shock at all that she'd risen quickly through the ranks. Indree had always excelled at anything she wanted to excel at.

Indree didn't answer. Instead, she strode across the

small waiting room and knocked firmly on the inner door.

"Enter," came a voice from the other side.

"Come on," Indree said, and beckoned to Tane and Kadka. "Don't do anything else stupid, and maybe I won't be throwing you in a cell at the end of this." She pushed open the door and strode through.

Kadka leaned close to Tane, grinning. "Think she likes you," she whispered.

"She used to," Tane answered quietly, and followed Indree in.

Tane had been in the chancellor's office only once before, after submitting his dissertation, and that meeting had ended in his expulsion. He very much hoped this one went better. The office was much as he remembered, huge and well-appointed, decorated with impressive artwork and artifacts of historical meaning to the University. One piece in particular drew his attention, one he didn't remember from the last time: a bronze sculpture against the northern wall depicting an archaic mage's staff extending upright through the center of a crown. The Mage Emperor's sigil. If the piece truly dated from the time of the Mage War, it was some six hundred years old.

Inside, the deans of the University waited on either side of the chancellor's desk: Dean Greymond, of course, frowning sternly at Tane; Sorn Brassforge, the dwarven Dean of Artifice, scratching his short auburn beard uncomfortably; and Valis Orthea, the Dean of Invocation, a massive, flaxen-haired ogren woman who could have been sculpted from marble.

And sitting behind the desk was Chancellor Talain Nieris, a pale elven man with startlingly blue eyes and just a touch of grey in the black hair around his sharply pointed ears—the only sign of his three hundred and more years, a long life even for an elf. One of the elder scions of House Nieris, a Great House of the Senate, he'd been named chancellor of the University near a hundred years ago. The latest in a long tradition of elves in the position. Where most of the so-called magical races had some innate magical quirk—the instinctive illusory camouflage of the gnomish, or the stone- and metal-sense of the dwarven—elves were, in the eyes of many, the living *essence* of magic. Almost none were born without the gift of magecraft, and their long lifespans allowed them to master it in ways few others could. When the Senate of Houses appointed a chancellor, it was almost always an elf, and almost never a surprise.

"Inspector Lovial. Thank you for dealing with this so promptly." Nieris stood and nodded a polite greeting. He was impeccably dressed, in a deep purple longcoat with a ruffled silvery cravat at his throat. "And Mister Carver. How… unexpected, to see you here again." If he was surprised, though, it certainly didn't show on his face. He gestured to a number of chairs arrayed before his desk. "All of you, please sit. I understand we have much to discuss."

Tane took his seat, the brass cylinder tucked in his belt pressing uncomfortably against his back. He gestured at the sculpture of the staff and crown. "A bit of a controversial piece to have on display, isn't it?" The Mage Emperor wasn't remembered very kindly by history. The last ruler of the Estian Empire, his war to subjugate the magicless had shattered a dominion that once stretched all across Calene and parts of the southern continent of Anjica. It was in the aftermath of the Mage War that the Audland Protectorate had been founded, an island haven for the mages and magical races who had found themselves feared and hated across the Continent—whether they had sided with the Mage Emperor or not.

"I don't think so," Nieris said mildly, settling back into his chair. "They say that forgotten history is doomed to repeat. If that is the case, then the Mage War is worth remembering, is it not?"

"I suppose," said Tane. He still didn't like having to look at the thing. *Easy to dismiss when you* have *magic. It was the ones who didn't that he enslaved and killed.*

"In any event, we aren't here to talk about the past." Nieris looked to Indree. "Constable Inspector, if you would?"

Indree was still standing behind Tane and Kadka, her cap under one arm. "Of course, Chancellor Nieris. For the benefit of those of you who weren't there, Stooketon Yard sent me to meet with the chancellor about the murder. Shortly after I arrived he informed me of a triggered alarm spell in the primary artifice workshop. Considering that we had come to investigate the same location, I chose to respond in place of the University Guard. When we arrived, we found the scene in... considerable disarray. These two were alone inside. We searched them, but found no evidence of theft."

"The alarm *was* us," Tane offered. "I'll admit that. It must have detected me when I gave Kadka back her badge. But there was already someone in there. The real question is, why didn't *he* trigger it?" No apologies—if he had any chance of not being thrown off campus, begging wouldn't do it. Confidence opened more doors than contrition.

Nieris frowned. "Perhaps you should tell us this story from the beginning, Mister Carver."

It didn't take long for Tane to explain what had happened: the intruder, the portal, the wraith, and the smaller details in between. "And that's about everything," he finished. "Questions?"

Greymond was the first to speak, rubbing her fingers against her temples. "You promised you wouldn't... Spellfire, Tane, I *should* have the Inspector throw you in a cell."

"Allaea was my friend. Are you really surprised that I lied?"

Greymond sighed. "I shouldn't be, should I? But somehow I keep thinking better of you. I'm sorry, Chancellor Nieris. This is my fault. I never should have asked—"

"We can work out who is to blame later, Dean Greymond," said Chancellor Nieris. It was, Tane thought,

more than a little bit satisfying to see Greymond interrupted for once. "Right now I only want information." Nieris
turned to Kadka. "What about you, Miss... Kadka, was it?
What do you have to say for yourself?"

Most University Guard would have been cowed under question from the chancellor, but not Kadka. She just
stared back at him, her arms crossed. "Is not so bad, is it?
If we aren't there, no one knows this man comes back, or
how. No one finds—"

"Any of the information we have now that we didn't
before," Tane said, before she could mention the scroll
case. Kadka gave him a questioning glance, but she didn't
contradict him. "We know he used a portal to get in, for
one thing."

"So you said. That shouldn't be possible." Now Nieris looked to Indree. "Inspector Lovial, you saw evidence
of this wraith?"

"I did. They trapped it in an engine casing."

"Then I suppose we must believe your tale, Mister
Carver. Where there is a wraith, there must have been a
portal. You say it made a noise?"

Tane nodded. "A howl, with a kind of crackling,
groaning sound behind it. It made me think of ice."

"Like *tunvok*," said Kadka, and then, after confused
glances from all sides, "Animal. From Sverna."

"It might well have been," said Nieris. "I can't imagine the portal came from there—the distance is too
great—but such rifts are... deeply unstable. It isn't uncommon for random instabilities to draw sound through
the Astra from places half the world away." He laid a
finger against his chin. "But I don't see how this man
could have done it. I crafted the campus wards against
such spells myself, and I daresay there is no mage alive
with as much experience in portal magic." That was true—
Nieris had been university faculty for literal centuries, and
experiments with portals had been much less restricted in
his youth.

"What if there were no portal wards for him to by-pass?" Tane asked. "Would anyone have noticed if they'd already failed somehow? Portals aren't exactly common. It might have been decades since anyone tried to open one on campus."

It was Indree who answered. "We've already secured the workshop and begun testing the wards. I received a sending on the way here verifying that they are intact."

"Of course they are," Nieris said, rather haughtily. "Our ward maintenance is very thorough."

"Well, then, there's another possibility no one is going to like very much," said Tane. "Any of you four can cast portals on campus. I know you were together last night, but were all of you accounted for today?"

Dean Orthea didn't look offended so much as absolutely horrified—and her exquisitely sculpted ogren features made even that rather lovely. "You aren't suggesting... It isn't possible that one of *us* could have done that to Miss Hesliar, is it?" She was very much the clichéd representative of her people—gentle, sensitive, appalled by senseless violence. Rather cruelly ironic, Tane had always thought, considering their great curse: one of every three was born a brutish, barely sentient ogre that had to be sequestered in a sanctuary at the far south of the Isle.

"Of course not, Valis," Nieris said, in the bland, placating tone of a man who had dealt with such sensitivity a thousand times before. "Classes were in session during your... adventure, Mister Carver. Any number of students can account for the whereabouts of each of my deans. And I was meeting with Inspector Lovial."

"Then someone found another way through," said Tane. "There must be a loophole, some way to make the wards see an intruder as one of you. I'd recommend changing the portal wards until we know more, at least for the workshops. No portals at all, in or out. The only perfect spell is one that deals in absolutes."

"As much as I appreciate your insights, Mister Carver," Nieris said dryly, "keep in mind that you are here to be questioned, not to lead the investigation."

Tane seized the opening. "Sir, at this point I know as much about what happened as anyone. More than most. I saw the man who did it. Even Ree—er, Inspector Lovial can't say that. If you want this solved quickly, you *need* me."

Dean Greymond interjected almost before Tane had finished speaking. "Chancellor, I don't think—"

At the same time, Indree said, "Sir, I have to protest—"

Nieris silenced them both with a raised hand. "Interesting. Perhaps 'need' is a strong word, but then... you *have* found several flaws in our wards already, and provided information we would not otherwise have, putting aside the issue of your rather questionable methods. And I will admit you showed considerable courage and ingenuity in dealing with the wraith."

Again, Greymond cut in. "Chancellor Nieris, there is the University's reputation to consider. If Mister Carver is seen..."

"That ship is already well over the horizon, Dean Greymond," Tane said. "If I wasn't noticed on campus before, I promise you nobody missed me being marched here by the constabulary. Better to claim that you asked me here to assist than admit you let an expelled student— particularly *this* expelled student—gain access to a murder scene without permission. *Especially* if the Lady Protector is watching closely." That was something of a guess, but Greymond had suggested it might be the case earlier—and if it was, the University couldn't afford any embarrassing gaffes.

"You do make a compelling argument for yourself, Mister Carver." Nieris stroked his chin. "It may be prudent to keep you on, if only for appearances."

Indree shook her head. "With respect, Chancellor Nieris, I won't allow this. Murder doesn't fall under campus autonomy. This is firmly within the purview of Stooketon Yard, and I can't have anyone interfering in my investigation."

"Normally you would be correct, Inspector," said Nieris, "but the Lady Protector has taken an interest in this, as Mister Carver suggests. I spoke with her shortly before summoning you. She wants the matter resolved promptly, before anyone links it to the airship project. The launch is scheduled for the day after next, and it must not be delayed. I have been granted broad authority to speed the investigation along. Mister Carver, the University can offer you fifty staves a day—will that suffice?"

Indree caught Tane's eye with a glare and shook her head, but he wasn't about to pass up an offer like that. All personal investment in the case aside, he was lucky to make fifty silver staves in a given *month*. "That should be... adequate. I'll need a badge, though."

"And have you wandering the campus entirely unrestricted?" Nieris chuckled in mild amusement. "I admire the attempt, but I think not. It's one thing to hire you, and another to let you display University colors. Take what's offered, Mister Carver."

"Fair enough," Tane said with a shrug. "I had to try. We have a deal."

"Splendid."

Dean Brassforge had raised his head at the mention of the airship—he'd always been reserved for a dwarf, unless he was talking about one of his projects. "So you think they were after my airship spells?" He scratched at his beard. "I don't like that at all. She's supposed to fly in a few days."

"I imagine we'll find that it's unrelated, Sorn," said Nieris. "Lady Abena simply wants us to be certain. But there are a hundred other projects being worked on in that shop, and we have no reason to believe this tragedy wasn't about some personal matter."

"Actually, sir," said Indree, "if Tane's story is true, then we have to assume this man wasn't there to kill Allaea, or he wouldn't have had reason to come back. I don't think he was expecting her to be there. He must have been scared off when she screamed for the guards, and returned today to finish whatever he meant to do that night. That doesn't mean the airship project, necessarily, but those diagrams *are* kept in the section where Tane says he was looking."

Nieris didn't look greatly pleased, but he said, "A point well taken, Inspector Lovial. I'll trust you and Mister Carver to look into that. Now, if you will all excuse me, I must see to the banishment of this wraith, and I don't want to hold you up any longer. If you need anything else, I have asked Dean Greymond to act as the University's liason in this matter—her divinations should prove useful to you."

The deans were the first out the door, but Indree lingered as Tane and Kadka stood. It was only then that Nieris spoke again. "Miss Kadka, if you would stay behind for one moment, please?"

Tane exchanged a glance with Kadka as he left, but she only shrugged. *Spellfire, I hope I haven't got her in too much trouble.*

As soon as they left the chancellor's waiting room, Indree spun to face him. She didn't look happy.

"Indree, I know you don't want my—"

Indree pressed a finger against his chest, backing him into the wall. "I don't care what Nieris said in there. You aren't getting involved. I just saw my best friend with the *skin* burned off her face"—her voice quavered slightly there, but she didn't stop—"and I intend to find the man who did it. I don't know why you came back, but the last thing I need is you making a mess of things."

It was disorienting, having her so near. The last time her face had been this close to his, it had been for very different reasons. *Or maybe not. We always did argue as often as the other thing.* "I'm so sorry, Indree. When I heard that it was Allaea... I just wanted to help."

Indree's scowl softened, but only slightly. "So you said before. I wish I could believe that you still care that much, Tane, I really do. But how am I supposed to trust anything you say? I'll make it simple for you: I don't care if you take the University's money. Just don't get in my way."

The door opened behind them, and Kadka emerged. Indree backed quickly away from Tane, flushing slightly.

Tane straightened his waistcoat and turned to Kadka, attempting to appear as collected as he could manage. "What did he want?"

"To tell me I am not guard anymore," she said. "I let you steal badge and lied to hide it. Can't have that when security must be strongest, he says."

"That's hardly fair. I'll tell him it was my fault, he'll have to—" Tane moved toward the door.

Kadka blocked his way with one arm. "No. Won't help. Is done."

"She's right," said Indree. "The chancellor isn't going to overturn his decision for you, of all people." A short pause, and then, to Kadka, "I'm sorry he got you into this."

"Got into it myself." The corner of Kadka's mouth quirked upward. "Even if he starts it."

"Either way, take my advice: get away before he makes it any worse," said Indree. "Oh, and I had your knives delivered to the guard barracks. You can retrieve them there. I don't know what you need so many of them for, but they're legal enough." She gave Tane one last look, as if she might say something more, and then shook her head and strode away down the hall.

Tane watched her go, until Kadka stole his attention back with a nudge in the ribs. "*Know* she likes you now."

"How do you get *that* from what she said?"

Kadka tapped the pointed tip of her ear with one finger. "Orc ears. Hear what she says even before I come out. Too much feeling, for someone who doesn't care."

"Oh, she definitely cares, if you call wanting to break someone's teeth a kind of caring." Tane started toward the stairs, and Kadka kept pace beside him. "Look, Kadka, I... I *am* sorry it happened like that. I didn't think they'd blame you."

"Doesn't matter," she said. "Have new work now."

Tane raised an eyebrow. "You literally just walked out of his office. What work did you find in the past minute?"

"Helping you investigate." Kadka grinned. "He pays you too much. We can share."

"What? No. Look, I'm sorry about what happened, but Indree wasn't wrong. Associating with me isn't good for the reputation. I'll only get you in more trouble."

"Trouble can be fun," Kadka said, still showing her teeth.

"Kadka, I can't—"

"You don't tell them about case you found," she said. "You think I don't notice? I say nothing then, but maybe now I tell someone."

"So that's how it's going to be? I pay you off or you tell Indree I'm hiding something?"

"No," said Kadka, and she looked genuinely perplexed by the anger in his voice. "You pay me to help you, *and* I don't tell. Don't want money for nothing. Why not? Without me, you would be crushed under shelf already."

Tane sighed and spread his hands. "Fine. I suppose I don't have much choice."

She nodded, as if confirming something she'd known all along. "So. Where is case?"

They were in the stairwell now, hidden from sight on a landing between floors. Tane leaned out to check above and below, satisfying himself that no one was coming, and then he pulled the scroll case from his belt.

It was a brass tube about a foot long, with a cap at one end. Just below the cap were a series of five rotating copper bands, with a matching set at the far end of the tube. Both sets of bands were engraved with glyphs of the *lingua magica*, and a pair of small arrows showed where the glyphs were meant to line up. In the center of the tube, a green peridot gemstone was held in a copper setting, joined by inlaid copper lines to the bands on either side. Tane tested one band and it rotated with a click, putting a new symbol forward. He popped open the cap and looked inside. Empty.

"What is it?" Kadka asked.

"It's called a scrollcaster, or sometimes a forger's case," said Tane. "They're used to send or duplicate documents. You roll up some paper and put it inside, then turn these dials"—he indicated the glyphed copper bands near the cap—"to the glyphs of the caster you're sending to. Whatever is written on your papers is copied onto the ones at the other end. They're mostly owned by very important people sending things like state secrets—it's illegal to own one without a license, and they all have a set receiving address." Now he tapped the bands at the opposite end. "These bands mean it's black market. The glyphs at this end are meant to be engraved, impossible to alter without wrecking the caster. If you flip to a new set of glyphs after sending or receiving something, it breaks the Astral link. Makes it impossible for a diviner to trace."

Understanding lit Kadka's eyes. "You think he used this to copy some spell from workshop."

"Probably. It might be as simple as someone trying to steal privileged spell diagrams to sell on the black market. It's empty, which either means our mage had time to copy what he came to copy and put it back in the drawer, or we stopped him before he found what he was looking for."

"So what is plan? Can it tell us something?"

"If he sent something, he'll have changed the glyphs, so we probably can't trace where it went. But if we find the maker, they might be able to tell us who bought it. And if we're very lucky, they might be able to divine *what* was sent, if not where. That's why I didn't tell Indree. She'd have taken it away, and no black market artificer is going to talk to a bluecap."

"But they will talk to you?"

"I know someone I can ask. I don't know how much he'll want to say."

A wide grin stretched across Kadka's jutting orcish jaw, and there was a rather menacing twinkle in her eye. "Maybe I will find way to convince him." She nodded decisively. "Come." She started down the stairs.

Tane hastily stowed the scroll case in his belt and hurried after her. "Come where?"

"I will get my things, give back uniform. Then, we find your criminal."

CHAPTER SIX

IT WAS STRANGE, seeing Kadka out of her uniform.

When she'd been wearing it, there had been a certain air of University prestige about her—when Tane had taken her badge, he'd felt the little rush of satisfaction that always came with defying authority. Now, absent the sword and pistol and dressed in rough-spun trousers and a threadbare shirt with tattered suspenders over top, she looked like a girl from some country village visiting the capital for the first time.

Except that there weren't a great many orcs living in country villages in the Protectorate.

Her wide-eyed awe didn't do anything to dispel the impression, either. As they descended from the street into the crowded disc-tunnels, she craned her neck eagerly to catch a glimpse of the floating ancryst platforms approaching the station.

"You must have ridden the discs before," Tane said, nudging his way through the current of departing passengers. "Correct me if I'm wrong, but you've lived in Thaless for more than a day, haven't you?" The question came out sharper than he'd intended. He was still annoyed at the way she'd forced his hand earlier, and the discs made him nervous at the best of times.

"Yes," said Kadka. "But is always exciting, no? To ride floating stones in underground tunnels? This is kind of magic I come here to see."

Spellfire, how am I supposed to stay angry if she's going to be so... enthusiastic? The discs probably *were* impressive, he had to admit, if one weren't accustomed to them: a series of linked ancryst platforms suspended in mid-air in a copper-lined tunnel, metal and translucent green stone glimmering under silver-blue magelight. Atop each disc was a wood-and-iron passenger carriage, large enough to hold perhaps thirty people if they were packed very closely together—and they always were. Tane hated it, but he could see how it might appeal to someone else.

They squeezed into a carriage full of humans and elves and gnomes and kobolds and more: miners and dockworkers and laborers in clothes much like Kadka's, students in so-called "scholar's uniforms"—topcoats of University silver-on-blue over much cheaper trousers and waistcoats—and well-to-do merchants dressed in colored silks and velvets. There were no seats inside, just a number of metal poles to grip and a tight space filled with every sort of person that called Thaless home—and in the Protectorate's capital, that meant every sort of person there was. Too many people, and not enough room. Tane shuffled aside as a foot-tall sprite fluttered by on iridescent butterfly wings to land on the narrow ledge along the wall where others of its kind perched.

The ancryst platform lurched into motion underfoot, and Tane's stomach lurched along a second behind. Sweat beaded on his brow, and his fingers compulsively rubbed the watch casing in his pocket. Magelights set into the tunnel flashed by outside the windows, making the shadows inside shift rapidly from front to back as if the passage of time had accelerated along with the discs.

Kadka was forced in close by the crowd, standing near enough that those sharp wolf-teeth could have easily taken off his nose if she'd felt the urge. She wasn't looking at him, though, electing instead to peer around with sheer wonder in her yellow-gold eyes. More than a few people looked back, suspicious or curious or both. For all the Protectorate's diversity, orcs and half-orcs were still a rarity. She didn't seem to notice the attention, though, or didn't show it if she did.

After a short while, Kadka turned back to him. "You know about magic," she said, loud enough to be heard over the surrounding chatter. Loud enough to be heard a disc down in either direction, by Tane's estimation. "I wonder sometimes, how does this work? Is there spell to make it fly?"

"Not exactly," said Tane, swallowing his nerves so that she wouldn't hear his voice shake. "The discs are ancryst. I assume you've heard of it?" She hadn't seemed well-versed in the stone's properties when she'd discharged her ancryst pistol at an open portal.

"It moves by magic, yes?"

"It moves *away* from magic, more accurately. The tunnel is lined with copper conducting a magical field, which repels the ancryst from all sides. As long as the field is balanced, the discs hover in the middle." It made him feel a little bit better, somehow, to explain how the magic worked—as if talking about it aloud could keep the spells from going wrong. "There are artifacts in the front and back that project their own adjustable fields, pushing us in the direction we want to go or slowing us to a stop. It's more efficient than a levitation spell—magic with a specific purpose takes far more power to maintain than a simple field that doesn't have to do anything but exist. I'd bet a mid-sized topaz array could power a section of tunnels for a year."

"Why only here? I travelled through other places to come here. They have nothing like this."

Tane shrugged. "Practicality. It's expensive to dig tunnels all over a city and line them with copper. If it was done today, they'd probably use an ancryst-powered rail-car above ground instead. The discs were really just an experiment, from before we had ancryst engines. Actually, they were what *inspired* the development of the ancryst engine—an ancryst piston moves in its cylinder in a very similar way to how the discs move through these tunnels."

Kadka nodded slowly. "I can understand this, I think." She grinned, showing her teeth. An elven woman standing beside Tane flinched noticeably at the sight. "But maybe more fun when I only think it is floating."

"Magic always seems less magical when you learn how it works," said Tane. "Once you know how all the pieces fit together, it's easier to see where a little mistake could lead to disaster. But it's better to know. At least then you're ready for it when the worst happens."

"Makes you nervous, travelling this way?"

"Like I said, there are a lot of things that could go wrong. But it takes hours to walk anywhere in Thaless, so... I've gotten used to it."

"Not *so* used to it." She eyed the sweat on his brow with a slight smirk.

"I manage," Tane said, a little defensively. "Anyway, it's my turn for a question. There's something I wanted to ask you about."

"So you ask to ask?" She laughed. "Such manners in big city. Just ask. No danger in question."

"I've heard about orcs being hard to detect with divinations, but I'd never seen it before. I didn't think it would be so absolute. You didn't trigger that mage's detection spell, and the wraith didn't seem to care about you at all. Is that something you have to *do*, or is it just natural?"

"I do nothing," said Kadka. "In Sverna, we say orcs are too strong for magic to touch, but how can I know for myself when there is no magic there? And after I leave, mostly no one casts spells on me. At University when I talk to mages they say is hard to find me with some magic, but is all kind you call divination. I never *see* it. Wraith is first time I know there is truth there. But... I still hurt myself on ward." She rubbed the tip of her nose. "And mage's spell still throws me. Why is this?"

"I assumed you would know more than I do," said Tane. "I can only tell you what I've read. I've seen it written in a few places that orcs have a faint link to the Astra. Every living thing has an Astral connection, but it's apparently weaker for the orcish, or maybe naturally masked somehow. That would make it hard for divinations to find you—they seek people out through Astral channels. But it wouldn't stop anything physical. Like you say, we know that you can still be tossed around, or blocked by a ward."

"What if we find mage, then? Spells stopped me before. I want better fight next time."

"Good question." Tane hadn't ever had to fight a mage before, and neither he nor Kadka had any magic of their own. It was worth musing on. "In our favor, it's hard to put together a spell quickly, and most mages are academics, not fighters. I don't think our man was combat trained, or he might have managed more than a simple force wave. That's the best you'll see from most mages in a fight. Things like spellfire take focus and power and precise wording—harder to cast and easier to stop. The best way to fight him would be to silence him somehow. He can't cast if he can't speak, unless he's very quick at writing glyphs. Distraction works too. Get him to lose concentration and his entire spell could fail, or go off very differently than intended. Or... Orcs can see in the dark, can't they?"

"Yes. Is this useful?"

"Maybe," Tane said. "If you can get him in the dark, or maybe blind him somehow... He could still cast, but every spell is a request of the Astra, and it needs instruction. Not being able to just point and say 'that person there' makes it much harder to specify a target. He'd have to aim by guessing a direction. It would make us harder to hit, at least."

"Useful, then," Kadka said with a grin that fell abruptly into a thoughtful frown. "I am hard to see with spells, you say, but this mage is no orc. Why does the University not cast spell to find him?"

"It isn't that easy. To cast any targeted divination you need to either know the target fairly well or have a divination focus—something from their body, like blood or hair or a fingernail. Which there are laws about, for privacy's sake. We'd need a constable with a warrant. But we don't even have a face or a name, let alone a focus."

"What about case you found? That was his."

"A diviner *might* be able to get some impression of past owners off of it," Tane admitted, reaching back to touch the scroll case in his belt and reassure himself it was still there. Pickpockets weren't unheard of on the discs. "But it's black market, so it will be masked—purposely passed between enough people and magical signatures to throw off any object reading. And anyway, divining anything outside the present is unreliable. Most of the time it just gives some vague vision, and the interpretation is as much about the diviner's bias as any real information. It's an option if we run out of others, but I'd rather not rely on it."

Kadka cocked her head. "For man who knows so much about magic, you don't like very much. Why?"

"I don't dislike it. I just don't *trust* it. And neither should you. Magic can be useful, but don't forget to look for the flaws. Better to trust yourself than a spell."

"Is good to trust in self. But good to use what is useful, too."

"I'll keep that in mind," said Tane. "Right now, though, the most useful thing is going to be finding whoever made the scrollcaster." He staggered against Kadka as the discs began to slow. "And on that note, it looks like we're here." *Thank the Astra.*

The familiar smells of salt and fish greeted Tane's nostrils as they climbed the stairs into daylight. The cawing of gulls rang from above. The disc-tunnels emerged near the Porthaven fish market, and the waters of the Audish Channel stretched out ahead, late afternoon sun shining off murky water between the hulls of dozens of anchored ancryst ships. It wasn't exactly beautiful, but it was always a welcome sight coming out of the tunnels.

Across the harbor, the towering scaffold around the airship's rigid envelope monopolized the shipyards, and the view. The outer skin—some artificer-made cloth with a shimmering finish—reflected the sunlight so that Tane had to squint to look at it. Over the months, he'd watched the envelope progress from a skeletal frame to a long, smooth ovoid, nearly finished now with only two days until its first flight. Below, the body of the ship rested in drydock, a lightweight wooden hull with a skeleton of steel, mounted with a pair of gleaming brass ancryst engines. Tiny figures crawled over the scaffolding and the body of the ship, making final adjustments, and Tane knew there were more that he couldn't see—at this distance, the diminutive sprites were entirely invisible, but dozens of them would be flitting about the higher parts of the scaffolding, their wings allowing them to work in relative safety.

"Hard to believe it will fly." The awe was back in Kadka's voice. "Something so big, how does even magic lift it?"

Tane only vaguely understood himself—the specifics were a fairly guarded secret. "Not all of it is magic," he said. "It's a little bit like a hot air balloon. They'll heat the air in the envelope with spell glyphs, but the lift that creates isn't magical. I'm not sure, but I'd guess there must be some levitation spells on the body too, or it would still be too heavy to fly—but nothing too strong, or they'd take too much power. That's where ancryst engines are useful. If you had to steer a ship that big with spells, they'd be so complex it would drain the gemstones in a day. It's a balance artificers have been trying to solve for a long time. Whether they got it right remains to be seen."

"You think it won't work?"

"I don't know. I haven't looked at the diagrams. It's going to be something to see if it does, but you won't catch me on board." Tane clasped Kadka's shoulder and steered her in the opposite direction, towards the fish market. "It isn't going to fly today, in any case. Come on."

Stalls filled all four sides of the little square, and gulls wheeled overhead, descending now and again to fight over discarded guts and fish-heads. People of all kinds and all sizes—save for a notable lack of elves, who for the most part kept to the better districts of the city—wandered up and down the market looking over the day's catch and haggling with the fishmongers. Most wore plain clothes, not far different from Kadka's, and Tane's frayed waistcoat made him feel almost overdressed. These were the residents of the Porthaven district itself, or perhaps Greenstone near the southern ancryst quarries, shopping for their dinner. Tane's class of people. His own cramped home—or rather the office that he happened to sleep in—wasn't far away. The wealthy citizens of the Gryphon's Roost didn't come to places like this. They had servants for that.

"This is black market?" Kadka asked, glancing over her shoulder one last time at the airship.

"*This?*" Tane had to laugh, looking over the run-down stalls. "No."

"What is funny?" Kadka half-grinned at his laughter, a picture of amiable confusion.

Suddenly, he could vividly imagine Allaea's voice—she'd always been the one to call him out. *You're being an ass, Tane. It was an honest question.* "Nothing," he said. "Sorry. It just occurred to me that crime in Sverna must be very different than what we have here." Svernan orcs eschewed magic altogether, by all accounts—they didn't have modernized magical cities like Thaless, or the thriving criminal enterprise that came with them.

Kadka shrugged, unperturbed as ever. "True. At

home when people break law, is all… smaller. Thieves, not whole market. But no need for sorry. Just explain."

"It's just… The black market isn't a place, if you're picturing something like the markets in Stooketon Circle. That would just draw the bluecaps right to them. It's more like a collection of people who know where to get things. Most of the illegal trade in Thaless *is* centered around the docks, though. Easier to smuggle goods in and out with access to the harbor, I suppose."

"Oh. So why here?"

"I know someone who might be able to point us where we want to go. Essik Tisk. He has a stall here, but it's mostly a front for peddling black market charms and artifacts." Tane didn't trust any spells he hadn't written himself, but it was illegal to cast from a diagram drafted without a University degree. He'd used Tisk more than once to commission custom spellwork from less-than-reputable sources.

Luckily enough, Tisk was working today—Tane spotted his distinctive blue-green scales from across the market. He was perhaps five feet tall, with green ridges running from the back of his head down to the end of his short, pointed tail. A heavy apron covered his chest, but beyond that he wore only a light cloth around his hips. Outside of uniformed professions, kobolds didn't much care for clothing.

"That's him," said Tane, nodding toward the stall. "Act like you're here for the fish. We'll work our way over."

Tane pretended to examine the wares at a few stalls, ambling gradually toward Tisk. Beside him, Kadka made a much less subtle show of it, loudly professing her admiration of the quality of the day's catch and drawing looks from everyone around them. *Spellfire, how is she so bad at this when I've seen her move without making a sound?*

"Carver." Tisk looked up as Tane and Kadka came near, and punctuated the greeting by chopping the head off a fish with his cleaver. "I'll be with you in a moment." He wrapped the fish, wiped his hands on his apron, and handed it to an elderly goblin woman, who thanked him and went on her way.

"I need your help with something, Essik," Tane said when the woman was gone.

Tisk turned his attention toward them and blinked slitted reptilian eyes up at Kadka. "Who's your friend? She's... loud." His tongue hissed on the 's' sounds. "And orcish. You didn't really think you'd go unnoticed with her around, did you?"

"I suppose not,' said Tane, "but it was worth a try. Essik Tisk, this is Kadka. Kadka, Essik Tisk."

Kadka clasped Tisk's hand, but she looked a little bit indignant. "I can be very sneaky. Just... different kind. Not so good at pretending."

"I'm sure," Tisk said, wincing at the strength of her grip. "So, what is it you two need?"

"I'd like to see what you have back there, if you don't mind," Tane said, nodding his head to the barrels of fish behind the stall.

Tisk beckoned them in. "Come right back."

Once they were somewhat shielded from view, Tane pulled the scrollcaster from his belt, keeping it low—out of sight of any wandering eyes. "I hoped you could help us find whoever made this. I admire the craftsmanship, and there's some work I need done."

Tisk glanced down at the scrollcaster for a moment, and then up again, swiping his forked tongue along his teeth. "Where did you get it?"

"In trade for some consulting I did. You seem like you recognize the work."

"I do." Tisk hesitated a moment, then hastily moved to his stall-front and pulled closed the shutters. "Come with me."

That was easier than it should have been. Essik was rarely so forthcoming—the black market survived through secrecy.

Tane had assumed that Kadka would need to show her teeth, at least. "Right now? I didn't think—"

"Come on, Carver. I can't leave the stall closed for long."

Tane glanced at Kadka; she put one hand on her waist, where he knew she'd tucked one of her knives, and gave him a slight nod.

"Lead the way, then," said Tane.

Tisk led them into a shaded alley behind the fish market, surrounded on both sides by brick-walled warehouses. Tane felt his pulse throbbing in his neck. *This was a bad idea. Alleys like this are where you get led right before you're murdered for asking the wrong questions.* His fingers found his watch casing, and he rubbed it nervously.

"Just up here," Tisk said, pointing at a blind corner up ahead.

Kadka stepped in front of Tane, her head slightly cocked. "Footsteps. Someone coming," she said.

Tane couldn't hear anything at all, but an instant later, three armed thugs rounded the corner to bar their way—a stocky dwarf with a forked beard and two impressively muscled human men.

"What is this, Essik?" Tane demanded. Kadka grabbed for the kobold, but he darted out of reach, toward the approaching men.

"Sorry, Carver," Tisk said over his shoulder. "You're a good customer, but not *that* good." He sidestepped past the thugs and disappeared around the corner.

Tane whirled back the way they'd come, but there were already three more approaching from behind: a hook-nosed goblin, a pock-faced human, and a particularly mean-looking gnome. At Tane's side, Kadka tensed, shifting on the balls of her feet.

Ahead, the dwarf stepped ahead of the others, holding a short brass wand in one hand. A daze-wand, Tane guessed—if he touched either of them with the end of it, an overwhelming surge of Astral energy would put them out of their senses for at least a minute or two. The two men flanking him both produced heavy cudgels.

"Easy now," the dwarf said, moving in close with his wand extended in front of him. "Don't give us any trouble and maybe you don't get hurt."

Tane raised his hands and took a step back. "We'll do whatever—"

Before he could finish, Kadka punched the dwarf in the throat.

CHAPTER SEVEN

TANE WATCHED IN horror as the dwarven thug stumbled back, clutching his throat. "Kadka, what are you *doing?*"

But Kadka's knife was already in her hand. Grinning savagely, she slashed at the arm holding the brass wand, and drew a crimson line across the back of the dwarf's hand. The wand clattered to the ground. Then, with something between a roar and a battle-cry, she bent low and tackled the man at the midsection. With surprising strength, she lifted him from his feet and *flipped* him over her shoulder into the three approaching from behind. The goblin dodged to one side, but the dwarf hit the human and the gnome full on, and all three collapsed in a tangle.

Spellfire, she might actually manage this. Tane snatched up the wand from where it had fallen—if this was happening, better to have a weapon than not.

The three thugs still standing closed in from both sides. Kadka's eyes went to the wand in Tane's hand, and she grinned wider. "Good! Get that one!" She jabbed a finger at the goblin. Before he could answer, she drew a second knife and charged the two big cudgel-wielding men ahead.

The goblin had a knife of his own, and he tossed it from hand to hand as he approached, sneering at Tane under a long, hooked nose. They were of similar height, but those lanky goblin arms gave the other man the advantage of reach. *This isn't good.*

Tane jumped back as the goblin lunged. He managed to twist out of the way of the knife, and jabbed blindly with his wand. The uninsulated copper tip brushed the inside of the goblin's forearm.

It was enough.

At the wand's touch, the goblin stiffened convulsively, and his knife fell from his hand. He staggered sideways into the alley wall and slid down it, a glazed look in his eye.

Definitely a daze-wand, then. That should keep him for a moment or two. But the fallen human and gnome had already squirmed out from under the dwarf, who was still gasping for air. Tane glanced at the peridot inlaid in the pommel of the wand—a very clouded, milky green. *Not much power left.* A daze-wand worked by pushing a powerful surge through the Astral connection of anyone it touched, which took a fair amount of power. He could daze one man before the gem crumbled, maybe, but not both. There was a way by, though, while they were still finding their feet.

Tane bolted past, looking back for Kadka. She was holding off both of the big humans; one clutched a deep slash across his bicep. "Kadka! Come on! Before they—"

And then he saw the others—three more thugs coming around the corner behind her. He snapped his gaze to the opposite end of the alley, and sure enough, another three emerged to cut off the path. Another goblin, green-brown with broad shoulders, pointed an ancryst pistol at Tane's chest.

"Drop your weapons!" the goblin ordered.

With his hand behind his back, Tane slipped the daze-wand up his sleeve and hoped it hadn't been noticed. He didn't want to get shot, but he wasn't about to throw away his only weapon. "I'm unarmed!"

The goblin jabbed the pistol's barrel toward Kadka. "You too! I said drop them!"

Tane looked over his shoulder; she was nearly beside him already, backing away from the advancing thugs with her knives still in hand. "Kadka!" he said sharply.

She glanced back, and saw the pistol. Her eyes narrowed.

"Boss wants to talk to you," the goblin said. "Drop the weapons and we'll bring you in safe."

"Can't say same for you," Kadka growled, and raised one of her knives, looking very much like she meant to throw it.

Tane lunged for her and caught her arm. "We'll come!" he said, and then again, more firmly, "We'll come with you." He gave Kadka what he hoped was a pointed look.

She stared back at him for a moment, and then sheathed her knives. "Good blades. Won't drop them." She raised a challenging eyebrow at the goblin with the pistol. "You want to take, come take."

The goblin frowned. "...Fine. Keep them. Boss wants you treated courteous-like. But reach for them again and we have a problem." He pointed further down the alley with his pistol. "That way."

The newcomers were already helping their comrades up, and several closed in around Tane and Kadka, escorting them rather firmly in the direction the pistol-wielding goblin had indicated.

"When you said you'd help me investigate, you might have mentioned that you're *insane*," Tane hissed to Kadka as the thugs marched them down the alley. Most of them, he noticed, were still watching her with wary eyes.

Kadka didn't look very contrite. "How do I know they don't want to hurt us? Maybe still do. Or do you know where we are going?"

He didn't have an answer for that, so he said nothing at all.

After a few twists and turns through the back alleys of Porthaven, they descended a staircase down from street-level to the faded basement door of an old brick building. One of the thugs knocked a particular pattern, and it swung open. As Tane passed through, he felt the hair-raising tingle of a ward sweep over him. Apparently they'd been granted access, because it didn't stop him, or Kadka.

Inside, the basement was considerably less run-down than it had looked from without. Warding glyphs were inscribed on copper plates in corners along the top of the wall, presumably linked to a power source somewhere out of sight. Near the door, elegantly set magelights illuminated a small library stocked with rather unusual magical texts: all of them were quarter-sized. Beside the shelves, two generously padded armchairs sat before a four-foot-high pillar furnished with a doll-sized chair and reading table. Atop the table, a tiny book had been left open—still over-scaled even at quarter size, but ancryst presses didn't work much smaller. It was clear at a glance that the little dais had been designed for a sprite.

Further back, an assortment of workers bent over a series of worktables much like the ones in the University's artifice workshops. The tables were strewn with charms and artifacts in various states of completion, many being assembled even as Tane watched.

A tiny figure hovered over the tables on iridescent wings, flitting from artifact to artifact. "No, no. We'd have to charge too high a price for gold-infused ink. For a one-time charm, the stability will be more than—"

"Boss?" The goblin put away his pistol with a sheepish look. "We brought them."

The sprite looked up. Oddly enough, the upper half of his face was covered with a deep green masquerade mask worked in fine gold and silver filigree. "Ah, welcome, welcome!" he said with the delight of a man greeting long-awaited guests. "Please, sit down! Make yourselves comfortable!"

Tane and Kadka were escorted to the larger armchairs, and Tane obediently sat down—they were still surrounded by armed men, and he didn't want to make anyone angry. Kadka was less willing, but when Tane glared at her, she took her place in the other chair.

The sprite fluttered toward them and landed on the dais, putting himself at close to eye-level. He looked nothing like the dangerous criminal Tane had expected. Quite the opposite, really: one tended to imagine sprites frolicking in glades with creatures of the forest, not selling illegal goods. And this one looked particularly ill-suited for it, with his exceptionally ample belly and that round-cheeked smile, so wide that it nearly split his face in half. Even his clothes weren't right. He was dressed like a gentleman of leisure, in a fine waistcoat and trousers of a deep green that matched his odd mask.

"Bastian Dewglen, at your service," the fat little sprite said, bowing enthusiastically. "I do apologize for the inelegant means by which you were escorted here. My friends were *meant* to extend every courtesy, but it seems things became rather... muddled. You must understand, in my line of work I have to be careful of those who come asking questions. Hence the mask!" He gestured to it and chuckled, as if quite taken with his clever disguise. "And the false name, which I regret to say is not my own—I've grown quite fond of it." He gestured to a gnome woman waiting nearby, a foot shorter standing up than Tane was sitting. She produced a small pair of scissors and started toward them.

Kadka was halfway out of her chair and reaching for her waist before the woman had taken her first step.

Bastian halted the gnome with a raised hand. "Ah, I must apologize again! I can see how this would appear untoward. But I assure you, it is only a bit of insurance. It won't hurt at all!"

"It's fine, Kadka." Tane offered his hand to the gnome woman. It wasn't hard to guess what she was looking for. "They just want a divination focus. Like I was telling you about before." There was an implicit threat there—*tell anyone about me, and I'll find you*—but that was better than an explicit one. The little sprite's friendly enthusiasm wasn't enough to make Tane forget the dangerous men standing guard all around them. *And if the scrollcaster is his work, he might have been the one behind Allaea's murder.* More likely he'd only sold the caster to someone else, but more wasn't out of the question. A black market spellmonger might have buyers eager to obtain highly guarded spells.

"Very astute!" Bastian said, clapping his hands in approval. "But I would expect nothing less from Tane Carver—the very man who bamboozled the University for years! You're right of course. I haven't much stomach for hurting people just to keep my little lair a secret, and I'm pleased to say no one has yet forced me to resort to anything so distasteful."

The gnome took a clipping from Tane's thumbnail and slipped it into a small glass vial, which she handed to Bastian as he spoke. Tane showed Kadka his hand to demonstrate the lack of injury, and she relaxed slightly into her chair.

"You know me?" Tane asked Bastian as the gnome woman moved on to Kadka.

"Of course! I make a point of knowing all the most interesting characters in Porthaven, and you were rather prominent in the Gazette for a time after your grand reveal. I was able to procure a copy of your dissertation—a very interesting read. I admire how far you went to prove your point. An honor to meet you at last, an absolute honor." Bastian turned to Kadka, and fluttered closer. "But who is your lovely friend? I must say, my dear, you are absolutely *intriguing.*"

The gnome woman was nervously clipping some fur from the back of Kadka's hand; Kadka bared her teeth in what could have been a grin or a snarl. The woman shrank away with a small lock of fur in hand, instinctively camouflaging herself to blend with the colors of the workshop behind.

Kadka watched the gnome's glamored retreat with some interest, and then glanced at Bastian as he drew near. "I am Kadka." She cocked her head at his obvious fascination. "Is something on my face?"

"Not at all, except perhaps for a lovely smile." Bastian's round cheeks rose into a broad smile of his own beneath his mask. "Forgive me for staring, but you are a wonder, my dear Kadka. I expected Mister Carver, but the warning charm I supplied Issik with failed to sense you at all. Even looking at you now, I can't sense so much as a *hint* of Astral presence! I have dealt with orcs who were hard to detect, but never quite so invisible. Something in the way orcish blood and human mix, perhaps? There are so few half-orcs, I can't imagine it's ever been researched." It was an interesting question. Tane had no way to check on his own, but Kadka's Astral masking did seem stronger than it ought to be.

Kadka shrugged. "Don't know. You are mage, not me."

"Ah, a mystery then! What a delight!" Bastian clapped his hands merrily. "Needless to say, my friends were quite surprised to see you in that alley without warning, let alone to have you fight back so skillfully. I am *deeply* impressed, on both counts. You aren't looking for employment, perchance?"

"Not now." Kadka glanced sidelong at Tane. "Maybe soon."

"Then I shall not stop asking! Expect a sending... hmm, I wonder." He picked up the small vial the gnome had placed on his dais—quite large in his little hand—and squinted at the tuft of Kadka's fur.

Kadka started in her chair and jerked her head around as if she expected to see someone behind her. "Who is there?" She smacked her ear with one hand, and then looked back at Bastian, as nonplussed as Tane had yet seen her. "Is... is your voice? In my head?"

Bastian chuckled. "Only a simple sending. I apologize, but I had to check." Sendings were a kind of divination, like any magic that sought a target through the Astra—apparently a divination focus was enough to locate Kadka even through the masking of her half-orc blood.

A brief silence, and then Kadka cackled aloud at something Tane couldn't hear. "You are funny, little man. But for today, I need no work."

"A pity," Bastian said. "But hope remains for another day! Now, if you won't accept my offer, I suppose it is time we discussed why the two of you are here. Something to do with the tragic events at the University last night, I expect?"

"You're… well informed," said Tane. "How do you know about that already?"

"Sendings travel quickly, my friend! In this city, no secret lasts much longer than it takes for the bluecaps to arrive. And your own presence hardly went unnoticed, either. But I can't imagine what you think I had to do with it!"

Tane produced the scrollcaster from behind his back. "This is your work, isn't it? It was found at the scene."

Bastian flitted to the arm of Tane's chair and examined the brass case. "Mine, certainly. Notice the peridot? Something of a signature. I find the balance of power and affordability quite ideal—and I am somewhat fond of the color!" He beamed broadly and patted his green waistcoat. "Now, if I might surmise: you are wondering if I sent someone to relay certain highly valuable spells to me via this scrollcaster. Spells, perhaps, relating to the majestic airship being constructed across the harbor?"

"It… has been suggested," Tane said cautiously.

"Well put your minds at ease! I may be a criminal, but I am also a patriot! Where else could I live as I do but in the Protectorate? In Rhien I would always be watched; in Belgrier my kind live in ghettos, hardly suited to free trade. And let us not forget Estia, where non-humans are stopped at the border. No, I support Lady Abena and her airship wholeheartedly. A more prosperous Audland benefits all of us!" He laid a finger alongside his nose and gave an exaggerated wink under his mask. "And of course, my business will hardly suffer from increased trade with the Continent. I may not wish to *live* there, but where magic is restricted, magical goods sell at… rather exorbitant prices."

Tane was inclined to believe him. There was no sign that the little man was lying—whatever else he was, he genuinely considered himself a devoted citizen. "Then I'm sure you'll be happy to help us. Can you tell us who bought this case?"

There, Bastian hesitated. "Now that is a delicate matter. I can hardly expect my business to prosper if it becomes known I am willing to reveal the names of my customers."

Tane leaned forward in his chair. "Can you expect it to prosper if the bluecaps start looking into what your product was doing in the workshop?" No need to mention that the bluecaps didn't actually *know* about the scrollcaster. "And they certainly will. They are under some pressure to resolve this quickly."

Bastian wrung his hands and paced along the arm of the chair, fluttering his wings erratically. "Oh dear. I was worried about that. I *do* want to help, of course, but…"

"Bastian, the Protectorate needs you. Lady Abena is very concerned about this—I was brought in under her authority." That was stretching the truth more than a bit, but Tane thought he had the measure of the man now—a representative of the Lady Protector could be just the person to convince him. "I believe you when you say you're a patriot, and a patriot answers when his country calls. Do the right thing."

Bastian puffed out his chest and bobbed his head enthusiastically. "You're right, Mister Carver! This is no time for selfishness! A girl has been killed, and the future of the Protectorate is at stake! Never let it be said that I quailed from my duty to my homeland!" He rose into the air, and beckoned them to follow. "Come, come! Bring the scrollcaster!"

Tane and Kadka followed him across the workshop, and as they passed, both of them examined the various artifacts spread across the tables—Tane with mild interest and Kadka with open curiosity. Charms, mostly: spells written on rolls of paper no bigger than Tane's little finger, wax-sealed and set with a small gem or crystal—rarely more than a quartz shard. When the seal was broken, the gem was consumed to power a single-use magical effect. There were dozens of them, identified in plain Audish on their seals: darkness charms, flash charms, shield charms, repulsion charms, and more.

Bastian led them to a small pillar at the back, much like the one in the library area. Atop it sat a small worktable covered in sprite-sized tools. He landed behind the little table and gestured toward it. "Place it here, if you will."

Tane laid the scrollcaster down on the table—it was rather too long, extending over the edge on both sides. Too large for the little sprite's hands, too, but Bastian uttered a spell and the brass tube levitated into the air, moving as he directed. With various instruments, he began to probe the dials and gemstone. And as he worked, he talked. "I remember the lad. He came in perhaps two weeks ago. I don't have much to tell you. He wore a... a kind of cowl that covered his face, and he gave no name. He paid a high price to waive the requirement of a divination focus, as well. I didn't think much of it, at the time— customers often want to keep their identities hidden, and I *am* a businessman."

This can't be a dead end. It's all I've got. "Is there *anything* you can tell us that might identify him?"

"He may have been a student at the University. He was young, I think. He fidgeted a great deal. Educated in magical matters by the way he spoke, but he didn't give me the impression of great experience."

"That's useful. Anything else? Did he buy anything besides the scrollcaster?" By way of example, Tane picked up a brass ball a little smaller than the palm of his hand from the table of charms. The clockwork key jutting from one side identified it as a charmglobe. A charm placed inside could be activated at a short delay set by winding the key. When it wound down, the ball would open and a brass lever within would break the charm's seal, activating it. And as an added benefit, the brass insulated whatever was inside against detection spells. Quite illegal, outside of the Protectorate's military—they served little purpose besides weaponizing charms. He tossed it absently from hand to hand a few times.

"No devices or artifacts," said Bastian, "but a number of components which might have been used for the construction of any long-term spell. Wards or the like." He set aside his tools with a sigh. "I had hoped, but... there's no way to trace where the caster sent last, I'm afraid. The sending and receiving glyphs have been changed. But I may yet be able to recreate what was sent, if you leave it with me."

"How long?"

"Two days, perhaps."

Kadka eyed Bastian with suspicion. "How do we know you don't just keep, tell us nothing?"

Bastian put a hand to his chest and fluttered his wings. "My dear Kadka, you wound me to my core! I thought we had an understanding! How can you think I would lie to you?"

She grinned. "Like you, little man. Doesn't mean I trust you."

"Beauty, strength, *and* wisdom," Bastian said wistfully. "If only I could convince you to lend them to my service. But I'm afraid all I have to offer you is my word."

"Then it will have to be enough," said Tane. If Bastian was up to something, he was an extremely credible liar, and either way the scrollcaster wasn't much use without him. "But as soon as you find anything, I want to know. You shouldn't have any trouble contacting us with a sending."

"Of course, of course!" Bastian enthused, fluttering from his table. "Is there anything else?"

Tane glanced at the charmglobe in his hand, and then at the charms spread across the worktables. With one notable exception, he'd been in more danger today than ever before in his life. It wouldn't hurt to be better prepared next time. *I'd rather not rely on someone else's spells, but... what did Kadka say? Good to use what is useful.*

"I might need a few things," he said.

CHAPTER EIGHT

———

"YOU COULD HAVE gotten us *killed*," Tane insisted, walking beside Kadka down the darkened street.

"But if they come to kill us, maybe I stop them," she said. "You would not be so angry then."

Tane sighed. It was pointless to argue with her. He hadn't known Kadka for long, but one thing was already clear: she didn't waste much time on doubt. "Just... let me try to talk to the next people who attack us, maybe."

She shrugged. "We will see. Some things, talk does not change."

That was probably the best he was going to get, so he let it be.

Evening had descended, and what sinking light remained in the sky couldn't force its way into the cracks of Porthaven's narrow streets and alleys. In the poorer districts, magelight had yet to replace the cheap oil-fuelled street lamps, dim and flickering and spaced so far apart that they served little purpose but to spoil Tane's night vision. And it didn't help that he was distracted, thinking about what Bastian had told them.

"Watch out," said Kadka, and nudged him around a pothole. She had no trouble with the dark—orcish night vision was evidently quite strong. "Thinking instead of looking, yes? About masked mage? Where to look next?"

Tane nodded. "It makes some sense if he's a student, like Bastian said. We know he can use magic, and he seemed to know what he was looking for and where to find it, which implies some knowledge of the University. It doesn't explain why he had a badge that got him into the room, though. A graduate student might have had access for a project, but that would only have worked the first time. When you and I caught him, the wards were set to keep student badges out. The only people who should have been able to get in were constables, heads of the University, and the Guard."

"But guard has no mages, and deans all have other stories."

"Right. And a constable would have been better trained in combat magic, among other things. Which doesn't get us anywhere. If we assume the badge was stolen by a student—I got in with yours, after all—it opens up possibilities. But even with a badge, if he somehow found a way to open a portal into the workshop, he'd need a place to cast it from. He couldn't do it anywhere on campus without being noticed. The components he bought must have been to cast new wards on a bolthole somewhere, and to prepare his portal."

"So maybe we look for student who is gone too much in last weeks. Warding lair, making plans."

Tane nodded. "Exactly what I was thinking. They'll have attendance records at the University. It's a start, at least. But I still can't figure out how he opened the portal."

"Yes, yes," she said. "Very strange." There was something cursory to it, like she'd stopped listening. Her head was slightly cocked.

"Kadka, what—"

"Pretend nothing is wrong," she whispered. "Hear someone following. On roof."

Tane forced himself to keep walking at the same

pace. "Could it be one of Bastian's?" he asked under his breath. But he suspected they weren't so lucky. There was no one else in sight in either direction—this would be the perfect time and place for an ambush.

"No. Would have heard sooner. Coming from other side."

Tane felt for the stolen daze-wand tucked into the back of his belt under his waistcoat, still probably good for one more charge. If he was lucky. His other hand slipped into his pocket, searching for the charms and charmglobe he'd bought from Bastian. All at a steep discount, of course, for a representative of Lady Abena, but still he'd only been able to afford three charms: shield, flash, and darkness. They all felt the same, just sealed rolls of paper. There was no way to identify them by touch. Surreptitiously, he drew one out and glanced at the writing on the seal, hoping for the shield charm. But it was too dark—he couldn't read it.

And then, suddenly, there was light, silver and blinding.

Before he understood what was happening, Kadka sprang into motion, pushing him to his knees behind her. Bright silver flames flared from the rooftop. She half-turned, leaning over Tane and shielding her face.

A gout of spellfire roared across her back.

"Kadka!" Tane shouted. He pulled out a charm, read the seal by the pulsing silver light. *Shield. Thank the Astra.* He crushed the seal in his fist, and a shimmering barrier of force surrounded them.

Silver fire licked along the outside of the shield for an instant longer, and then blinked out as if it had never been there. Tane leapt to his feet and spun to face Kadka, expecting the worst. Blackened flesh melting from cracked, crumbling bone. Just like Allaea. *Not that. Not again.*

She was entirely untouched. The flames hadn't burned her at all. She looked as surprised as he was, probing her shoulder where the flesh should have been seared away.

Impossible. Her masked Astral link might protect against divinations, but spellfire was physical. It should have killed her. *Unless... he was aiming for me.* Spellfire only burned what it was told to burn—their attacker must have been too precise in naming his target. He hadn't predicted Kadka getting in the way. *But* she *had no way of knowing that.*

As soon as she realized she was unharmed, Kadka drew a knife from her sleeve with a flick of the wrist and hurled it through the darkness at the source of the spellfire. The blade passed silently through the shield—the charm only kept things out, not in.

No sound, no scream. An instant later, the sound of the knife skipping across the rooftop.

"Come out!" Kadka shouted. "*Poska!* Fight me where I can see!"

No answer.

Not aloud, anyway.

A sudden pressure in Tane's ears, and then a voice spoke in his head. *"Forget the scrollcaster. Leave this investigation alone."* The mage had to be near, still—without sufficient familiarity or a focus, finding an Astral signature to send to or divine from was only possible at close range. Tane swept his eyes over the rooftops, but he couldn't see anything in the dark. *"This is your only warning. The next time, you won't be so lucky."* Clear as diamond, an image flashed across his mind: a door in a brick-front building, the same as any of the identical narrow single-room homes on either side, joined together in one long row. Only the number painted on the letter-box by the door distinguished it from the others.

17.

His number. The office he rented near the docks.

Then, a burst of intense pain, like a spike driving through both temples. "Ahh!" Tane bent over, gripping his head in both hands.

"Carver?" Kadka knelt in front of him. "What is wrong?"

The intensity faded as quickly as it had come, but it left a pulsing ache behind. "N—nothing. Just... a sending. Is he still..."

Kadka shook her head. "Gone. Heard him running. Maybe wasn't expecting... this." She gestured at the shimmering barrier around them.

Tane straightened up and rolled his head from side to side. It didn't help the headache. "Kadka, you... you jumped in front of spellfire for me." He paused, and then, "Do you have any idea how *stupid* that was?"

Kadka shrugged. "Felt like thing to do. Why doesn't it burn?"

"It would have, if he'd been any smarter about phrasing the spell! If he hadn't specified me as the target, you'd be dead!"

"I should have let you try to talk to fire instead?" She flashed her wide, toothy grin.

"No, that's not..." Tane let the sentence drift away unfinished. Just like before, there was no point in arguing with her. His head hurt and he could still feel his heart beating against his chest, but he had to laugh. "I mean, *thank you*. Obviously. But please, in the future, try not to get yourself killed on my account."

"Don't stand in front of spell, then," Kadka said. "What was sending? Way you shout, it sounds painful."

Tane frowned. "He wants us to drop the investigation. Forget the scrollcaster, he said. Then there was an image of the place where I live, and... pain." Just thinking about it made him wince.

"Pain? This is possible? Why not do *that* when we fight him?"

"He'd have to be focused on the Astra to send. When you see that distant look in a mage's eyes, that's what they're doing—looking past the physical world. Not ideal in the middle of a fight. But outside of one, just about anything can be sent. Words, images, emotions, sensations. Some of it isn't *legal*, but I don't think our mage cares very much about that."

"Talking of mage, we should not stay here. Don't know how long—" Before Kadka could finish, the shield blinked out of existence. "Ah. Not long. You have place to go?"

"My office isn't far," said Tane. "We'll be safe there."

"You mean place he showed you?" She raised an eyebrow. "One place where he *knows* to find you?"

"If he tries anything, he'll be disappointed. I'd trust my wards against any mage in this city. I designed them myself." He didn't keep them up unless he needed them—couldn't afford to replace the gems regularly—but this definitely merited the cost.

"But—"

Tane didn't wait for her to finish. His head was still throbbing. "Come on," he said, starting down the street. "I need a drink."

CHAPTER NINE

————

"IT DOESN'T MAKE sense!" Tane threw the spell diagram down on his desk and took another swig of whiskey—no aged Belgrian, but the cheap local stuff dulled the pain in his temples just as well. "I can't find the problem. He shouldn't have been able to open that portal."

The ward diagrams had been delivered to his letterbox while he and Kadka were out, as Dean Greymond had promised. Tane had been looking them over for the past quarter hour or so, but he couldn't see the answer he was looking for, and he was getting frustrated. Usually he could find the flaw in a spell at a glance.

"You are sure there is one?" Kadka asked. She sat across from him in the flimsy chair he kept for clients—not that he had many of those—with her feet up on his desk. There wasn't much else in the room, just a few cabinets, a single magelight lamp casting silver light from the corner of the desk, and a folding screen at the back that hid his mattress from sight. Being a 'magical consultant' without any magic or University honors hadn't proven particularly profitable.

"Like I told you before: the flaw in all magic is the mage. They always miss something. Sometimes it's minor enough not to matter, or obscure enough that it will never come up, but it's always there. And there has to be a hole in these portal wards, or he couldn't have done it. I just can't *find* it."

Kadka pulled the diagram to the edge of the desk with one foot and blinked at the glyphs for a moment. "Nonsense to me. Why not write with letters?" Leaning back, she took far too large a swallow of her own whiskey, and didn't so much as flinch as it went down.

"To avoid the kind of problem I'm looking for. Most languages are a clumsy patchwork, thrown together by necessity. You *could* use them for spells—the Astra doesn't care—but you risk all manner of problems with connotations and identical spellings for entirely different things. The *lingua magica* was designed to be precise. A unique word for everything, a unique glyph for every word. Perfect for casting, in theory, except the person choosing the words can still be an idiot. Nothing can fix that. There's *always* a flaw."

"How do you find, usually?"

"Most of the time it's easy. Find the flaw in the mage and you'll find the flaw in the spell. Are they lazy, arrogant, prejudiced? Figure that out and you know what mistakes they'll make. Those old folktales about some ward that 'no man shall pass' and then a woman does? In real life that's not some epic destiny. It's because someone with a low opinion of the opposite sex just entirely forgot to consider them. The thing is, though, as far as I can see, *this* ward is too simple to break." He traced a line under the glyphs with his finger. "This essentially says 'no portals into or out of the University campus unless made by the chancellor or one of the deans'. That's fairly absolute." Tane took another sip and winced against the burning in his throat. "But there has to be something. And I'm going to find it."

"You are so sure only you can? Why not your Inspector Indree? Or University mage? They must know magic same as you, yes? Could tell them what we find. Too late for them to take scrollcaster away now."

"No one born with magic is ever going to see through a spell like I can," Tane said. "That kind of power, you start to forget it's not perfect. You stop seeing the flaws even when you're looking for them. Even Indree. She's always been brilliant, but she's not going to solve this. She's a mage. It has to be me."

Kadka cocked her head at him, curiosity glinting in her yellow eyes. "And you don't think to quit? Some men would, after mage throws fire at them."

"If he wants to stop me, it just means I'm close to something. All the more reason to keep looking."

Kadka laughed. "This is why I like you, Carver. But there is more, I think."

"Of course there is. Allaea was my—"

She shook her head. "Vengeance for friend I understand, but is not all. You spend four years lying to University to prove you are better than mages, and still you talk about spell like enemy to fight. Is personal for you. Why?"

That was more insightful than he'd expected. *Maybe it's the whiskey. Speaking of which…* He took another gulp, and waggled a finger at her. "No, no, no. Everyone we meet has had something to tell you about me, but all I get to know about you is 'came from Sverna for magic'? I know a dodge when I hear it. No one is that willing to jump in front of spellfire without some reason. You don't get my story until I get yours. Fair is fair."

Kadka shifted her heavy lower jaw from side to side for a moment, considering, and then nodded. "Fine. I tell you, you tell me. But you try to get out of this, I find other way to make you pay. Yes?"

Tane raised a solemn hand. "I swear by the Astra, I'll keep my end." He probably owed her that much for saving his life, and at least this way he'd be considerably drunker when his turn came.

Kadka took her legs off the desk and sat forward in her chair. "Is not such a long story. When she is young, my mother leaves Sverna, like I do. Goes to Rhien, Audland, Belgrier. Sees many things. In Belgrier, she meets my father. He makes her pregnant with me. But he is human from wealthy family, and this is not so good in Belgrier."

"I can imagine." None of the nations on the Continent allowed mages or non-humans to live entirely free. Belgrier was neither the best nor the worst, but they were strict about segregation. For a wealthy Belgrian family, a son having a child by an orc would be an enormous scandal.

"His family has my mother put out of country. Never sees my father again. She does not want to raise me alone, so she comes home to clan. I grow up in Sverna. Is law to serve as soldier there for time when young, so I learn to fight, and to hunt food for clan." That explained some things—from what little information made it out of their borders, the Svernan army was said to train exceptionally skilled fighters. "But they think human blood is weak. Is… not always good life for me." Kadka took another long swallow of whiskey to finish her glass, and slid it across the desk to Tane. He refilled it and pushed it back.

"When things are bad, my mother teaches me tongues she has learned, tells of all the things she sees when she travels. Boats and carriages that move by magic, people with wings and dragon scales, cities lit after dark by silver light. One day, she says, I will see all of this myself. For a long time, closest I get is when I am hunting by border of Rhien and one of your ancryst trains goes by, far away over plains. But always I dream of lands where magic is real.

"Then my mother gets sick. She does not get better." Kadka dipped her head between her shoulders.

"I'm sorry," said Tane. "I… know what that's like." Absently, he touched the watch casing in his pocket.

"Thank you." Her mouth turned up at one side, revealing her teeth. "But is not your turn yet." She took another long drink, and then, "Without her, nothing is left to keep me there. So I go, like she did. Think I will travel world, see magic everywhere. Get away from place where they look at me and only see human."

"Did you ever try to find your father?"

"No," she said firmly. "He had chance. Could have fought for us, left with my mother. He is nothing to me. I leave for me, not for him. But... is not like I dreamed. Not so magical. Everywhere I go, they look at me like I don't belong. People say Protectorate welcomes all kinds, so I come across channel. It is... better, but still I see how people look at me. Even at University, they only let me join guard because I fight better than the rest. Beat them all, sparring. There is law here, I think?"

"There is," said Tane. "If you beat the other applicants, they'd have to take you. Can't turn you down for race—that's why the Protectorate exists. Although, ask any goblin, they'll tell you that people find ways around it."

Kadka nodded. "They are not so sad to see me go, I think. But they do take me, first. Is good to have work, and some in guard are friendly enough. And there *is* magic here, but not like dreams when I was little. There are discs, and people like I never see before, but mostly I just stand outside doors while they do magic on other side. And then you come, and steal my badge." She smiled—not her usual toothy grin, but something more wistful. "Today, I see more real magic than my whole life before. Portals and spells and silver fire. Like my dreams."

"Mages throwing spellfire aren't exactly the stuff dreams are made of. Nightmares maybe. My friend is dead, Kadka."

"I know. And I am sorry. I don't mean that it is good this happens. But today I feel like I have... purpose. Like this is what I am looking for. I want to find this man who kills your friend. See what he can do, with all his magic. And maybe next fight, *I* win." She shrugged. "Does this make sense?"

"Not really," Tane said. "But... I suppose I under-stand. If I'm being honest, it's... not *just* about Allaea for me, either." He sighed and took a sip. It burned all the way down. "I wish it was. She deserves that much. But it's not."

Kadka rolled her hand in the air. "Keep going, Carver. I tell mine. Your turn."

"I suppose I have to now." Another long pull drained his drink, and he poured another. It was keeping his headache at bay, and he was going to need it for this. "First thing, you need to know about my father. He's gone now, and my mother, but when I was younger, he was a conductor on the ancryst rail."

Kadka's eyes widened. "This means he drives it, yes? He must have been great mage."

"He wasn't. Or my mother. No magic at all. Mages cast the spells that make the trains run—other people do the everyday work of operating them. That's the problem. But that... that comes later." Tane reached into his pocket and took out his watch casing, a battered brass circle covered in old dents and scratches. "This was his. My father's, I mean. It doesn't work now, but he used it to keep the time on his route. He'd let me play with it, pre-tend I was a conductor myself. Sometimes my mother would take me to the station when he was due home, and we'd watch the trains come in. I loved it." For a moment, the memory made him smile, but it curdled just as quickly. He took another drink.

"When I was thirteen, he took us on a trip. His route went north into the country, and we were going to stay out there for a few days. I'd been on his train before, but this was the first time I was old enough to really take an inter-est in how it all worked. So the day we left, he took me up to the engine while they were still checking all the parts.

"I still remember everything. An aquamarine array for power, brand new without a hint of clouding. Steel pistons with ancryst cores. Everything polished to a shine inside a brass engine casing. He showed me all of it, every rod and bolt. All those men working on it, and my father in charge of all of them. That stays with me, more than anything." Another drink, longer this time. "He was looking right at it. All of them were. And they didn't see anything wrong.

"After, the artificers found that the spells pushing the pistons had been misaligned. Off balance. The train jumped the track at exactly the wrong place, crossing a ravine. Not many people came out alive." His hands shook as he pulled down the neck of his shirt, enough to show her the beginning of the scars that ran from his collarbone to his navel. "I had to be put together again by mage-surgeons. My parents weren't so lucky."

Kadka took in the scars with a solemn frown. "Awful. Carver, if telling is too hard…"

"No, we had a deal. And this was… a long time ago. It's fine." But he poured a third glass and took another long sip. The warm whiskey haze made it easier.

"This accident… this is why you don't like riding discs?"

Tane gestured wide with one hand. "It's why *everything*. My father and a dozen other men checked that engine piece by piece, and didn't see the problem. They knew everything about the mechanics of it. Nothing about the spells. And it was such a simple thing. There's nothing to it, just basic magic fields. The ancryst does all the work. I don't know if the mage was lazy, or stupid, or…" He sloshed the whiskey around in his cup. "Or drunk. But if *anyone* else had known what to look for, it wouldn't have happened. My parents didn't have to die. And it didn't even *change* anything. They died, and all anyone did was put a new mage in charge of maintaining the engine spells." He drained half his new glass in a single gulp. It didn't seem to burn so much anymore.

"So you go to University. Try to show them this."

He bobbed his head emphatically. "Except it wasn't that easy. I had no place to go, and no money to pay tuition. I was living in an orphan's home. Just fooling the

University wasn't good enough—I had to place high enough on the entrance exams to earn a scholarship with room and board. So I worked out every detail. Studied for years, figured out exactly how I would do it. Found ways to get my hands on the books and charms and artifacts I needed, legal or not. Practiced my sleight of hand until I knew every trick by heart. And as soon as I turned eighteen, I took the entrance exams.

"Before the written tests, they make you move a piece of ancryst, just to prove you can. I snuck in a charm to do it for me. Got it past all their detections. Not so hard—they don't know mundane tricks as well as magical ones." Tane flipped open his father's watch case. A coin-sized piece of cloudy green ancryst was anchored inside. No longer shielded by brass, it slid very slowly away from the magelight in the corner. "Palmed the stone as a momento. And it worked. I got the scholarship. Top marks on every test. I thought that would be enough. I was in, and when I graduated without magic, they'd have to listen. But you know how *that* ended." He snapped the watch case shut, shoved it back in his pocket, and took another drink.

"And this is why so many are angry with you? You lie about magic?"

"Like Dean Greymond, you mean? Absolutely. And she's not alone. When word got out, it was an embarrassment to the University, and a lot of people think that was the point. But Indree?" Tane rubbed the back of his neck. "That's different. When I was expelled, I didn't exactly tell her about it. We were… close, and I more or less vanished on her. And on Allaea, too."

Kadka narrowed her eyes. "This is *poskan* thing to do, Carver."

He didn't know exactly what that meant, but he knew it wasn't good. He raised his hands defensively. "I know. But Greymond and the chancellor asked a lot of questions before they threw me out. About who else knew. Being close to me was going to be a liability, and I didn't want anyone else dragged down. Thought it would be best if I just... left. Went as far as using divination masking artifacts the first few weeks, in case anyone came looking. It wasn't my best moment."

"No," Kadka agreed, still scowling. He couldn't blame her—she'd *just* explained how her father had abandoned his family.

Probably shouldn't have told her that part. "Indree really wasn't wrong when she told you I'm not the best person to be around." He sighed, took another drink. "All of this, with Allaea... I want to find whoever killed her, I really do. To make some kind of amends, even if it's too late. But it's more than just that. If I can help solve it..."

"Maybe people see worth of mages with no magic."

"Yes. Something like that. Spellfire, that's miserable, isn't it? She's dead and I'm worried about proving a point."

Kadka's face softened. "Not so bad. You still try to find her killer, just want to honor your mother and father at same time. Is not insult to your friend to want both." She smiled, surprisingly gentle. "Tell me what she is like, this Allaea. Is good to remember, maybe."

It might have been the whiskey, but that felt right, just then. Tane didn't fight it. "I met Indree first. We were fighting it out for top spot in most of our classes. At each other's throats most of the time, until... until we were at each other's throats in a different way, I suppose. Allaea was her closest friend. We spent a lot of time together, the three of us. Long nights studying, debating big ideas in their room in the dormitories. And it wasn't just 'any friend of hers' with us. Allaea and I got along right from the start. Which, if you knew her, didn't happen often.

"She *could* have been friends with anyone on campus, if she'd wanted. She was funny, pretty, an absolute genius at artifice. Elven, which... it shouldn't matter, but for some people it does. But she didn't have the patience. She expected the best from people and she wasn't shy about letting them know it. And she could be *mean*." He smiled fondly. "You know that way that some people can say the worst things, but it feels like a compliment?"

Kadka grinned. "I know this, yes."

"She was like that. Except if you got on her bad side... it could be *brutal*. The funny thing is, she was also as soft-hearted as anyone I've ever known. The kind of person who couldn't turn a blind eye when someone needed help. Spellfire, the things she'd say to chase off a bully. You wouldn't believe it. I once heard her call someone a 'quivering mound of putrid kraken pus'."

Kadka cackled long and loud. "I *like* her."

"So did I," said Tane. "So did everyone, even with the sharp tongue. People were always making advances, trying to get her attention. She *hated* it. An elf who looked like she did, they assumed she came from money or power. She didn't. But if they were decent about it, she'd let them down easy. If they weren't..." He laughed, remembering. "Well, you get the idea."

"Sends them away limping on broken pride?"

"Exactly," said Tane. "And she was *good* at it. I was on the wrong side of it more than once. Maybe you've noticed, but I'm told I can be a *tiny* bit arrogant, sometimes."

"Man who thinks he can best any mage in city?" Kadka put a hand to her chest in feigned shock. "No."

"Well, she never let me get away with it. But when I needed help, she was always there, too. When me and Indree argued—and we would *argue*—Allaea would usually tell me how to fix it. She knew Indree long before I did, and she always had the answer. She liked us together. 'There are a lot of idiots she could be with, and you're probably not the worst,' was how she put it. From her, it meant a lot." Tane ducked his head to wipe away the sudden moisture in his eyes. "I miss her. I... don't think I knew how much until..." He couldn't finish past the thickness in his throat.

Kadka raised her glass. "To Allaea."

Tane just clinked his glass against hers, unable to speak. He drained the rest of his drink in a single pull, and Kadka did the same.

Tane looked at the bottle for a long time, and then put his glass down. "I think I've had enough. If we're going to find who did this to her... I need to sleep. We can meet early—"

"Oh, I am staying," Kadka said, utterly matter-of-fact.

Tane froze in his seat. "Kadka, you don't think... This was nice enough, but we're not..."

She laughed. "You have too much to drink, Carver. Not like that. In case mage comes looking."

Tane felt his cheeks flush. "Oh. Right. Sorry."

"Is fine. I know is not me you want in bed." She raised an eyebrow suggestively. "Maybe tomorrow we impress Indree for you, yes?"

"That's... She's not..." But he couldn't come up with a convincing lie, so he didn't bother. "You don't have to stay. No one is getting by my wards, and I don't really have anywhere for you to sleep."

Kadka shrugged and leaned back, putting her feet up on the desk again. "Chair is fine." There was something about the way she said it that didn't leave room for argument. And it *did* make him feel a little bit safer, having her there.

"If you say so." He stood up, stumbled, and braced himself on the edge of the desk. The whiskey had hit him harder than he'd thought, and they'd been sitting a long time.

Kadka grinned. "Humans. Can't hold drink."

"Shut up." He touched the glyph to turn off the magelight on his desk, and traced a slightly crooked path through the dark to the folding screen at the back of the office. But before he collapsed onto his mattress, he turned back. "Kadka?"

She was only a suggestion of a shape in the dark, leaning back in her chair. "What?"

"Thank you." And then he let himself fall into bed, and remembered nothing more.

CHAPTER TEN

———

"AND JUST WHERE are you getting this information?" Indree demanded, glaring at Tane with her arms crossed. She wasn't wearing her constable's uniform today, just a charcoal topcoat over a white shirt and dark trousers, with her hair tied back behind her pointed ears instead of pinned up to fit under her cap. Plain enough that she could ask around campus without drawing too much attention.

"Yes, Mister Carver," said Dean Greymond. "You'll have to explain how you arrived at the conclusion that our murderer is a student, after you defended Mister Thrung so effectively yesterday." She sat behind her desk, frowning heavily. Indree had already been there speaking with her about the investigation when Tane and Kadka had arrived. "And while you're explaining, what is Miss Kadka doing here? I understood that she had been relieved of duty."

"She's not—"

"Yes, I'm aware she isn't here as a member of the Guard. What I am asking is, why is she with *you?*"

Tane glanced at Kadka for a moment, and shrugged. "Consider her… my partner, for now."

Kadka grinned at that. "Needs someone to look after him."

"A fair assessment," Greymond said with a very mild smirk. "Fine. What about the rest of it?"

"A student just makes the most sense," said Tane. "Before we even get to badges, the only people who could have gotten by the basic ward on that room are present and former students, faculty, staff, guard, and constabulary. We know it was a trained mage, so staff and guard are out—even if one of them had some latent gift, they wouldn't know the *lingua* or how to use it. I'm certain the man we saw was younger, and his spells weren't particularly polished, so student fits better than faculty or constable. I asked around with certain... less-than-savory contacts, and they tell me a man in a mask like the one Kadka and I encountered was seen buying black market components very recently." Still best not to mention the scrollcaster, not until he heard back from Bastian. "They got the same impression—young, and probably a student, by the way he spoke."

"Certain contacts?" Indree raised an eyebrow. "I need names if I'm going to use this, Tane."

"If I gave their names to a bluecap, they wouldn't be much good as contacts anymore, would they?"

"You expect me to just take your word?" said Indree. "Even if I was at all willing to do that, it isn't much to go on."

"Let me finish. We have to assume he wasn't buying those components to use on campus—any new wards would have been noticed, let alone a portal opening in the dormitories. And I can't imagine he found a way past the portal wards without some experimentation. He must have set up some sort of workshop in the city, and spent considerable time there. What we need to do is look for students who have been absent from class over the last few weeks."

She didn't look very happy about it, but Indree had never been one to ignore a well-reasoned argument. "So you suggest we go over the attendance records for everyone who missed a class or two? We can't question that many people without missing something important. One point of reference isn't enough."

Tane felt a smile tugging at the corner of his mouth. Despite everything, this felt like the way it used to be, sparring with her over magical theory or spell construction late into the night. The ideas on either side of those debates had always come out more refined than they had been going in. "You're probably right. I can tell you I'm sure he was human or half-elf by build, and male."

"Better, but still too many. If you'd said gnome, or dwarf, maybe, but human men leaves us with a list of near a thousand across all years, and hundreds will have missed a class recently." Indree prodded the side of her cheek with her tongue, the way she did when she was thinking, and then, "Dean Greymond, does the University—"

"Yes, we keep a record of students who are related to members of the University Guard, at least for immediate family. There are tuition benefits involved. Shall I have them ready that along with the attendance logs?"

Indree nodded. "And a full guard roster, so we can compare surnames. Whoever did this, they needed access to a guard's badge to get in, and they had to be able to get it back before anyone noticed it missing. That wouldn't be hard for a spouse or relative."

"Or a friend," Tane pointed out.

"True," said Indree. A pause, and then, "But the first… incident"—she tensed visibly there, even without mentioning Allaea's name—"happened past midnight. Less likely for a friend to be in your home at that hour unobserved. And we don't have any way to check for friendship. If this doesn't turn anything up, then I'll worry about expanding the list." She was as competitive as ever—couldn't let a point stand if she thought she knew better, which she usually did. There was something comforting about that.

"Fair enough," said Tane, and started for the door. "Let's go."

"No." Indree's voice was firm, and when he looked back at her, she shook her head. "You've been... more helpful than I expected, Tane, but I don't need you for this."

"The more help you have, the faster it will be to compare those records. And I can be useful when it comes to the questioning. You know I'm good at reading people. Please, Indree. I want to help. Allaea was important to me too."

Indree's eyes narrowed. "Don't you *dare* use her to—"

"Is not like that." Kadka didn't flinch when Indree's glare fell on her.

"You two met *yesterday*. What do you know about it?"

"Only what he tells me," Kadka said gently. "Your friend is woman I am sorry not to meet. I see his tears when he remembers her. Carver is good liar, but this was not lie."

Tane wasn't sure if he should be grateful or embarrassed. And Indree was staring at him again now. "The thing is," he said, "we'd been drinking—"

"Shut up, Tane," Indree snapped, and then shouldered past him to the door, yanked it open, and marched through. It had nearly swung closed when she stopped it with one hand and peered back in, scowling. "Are you coming, or not?"

———

Tane was beginning to worry.

They'd been at it for most of the day, and made little progress. Even the narrowed list left dozens of students to interview, and most could account for themselves during one of the intrusions or the other. The few who couldn't weren't strong suspects—there was no reason to believe they'd been involved, other than that the timing worked. *If we don't find something soon, Indree will never take me seriously again.*

"Who's next?" Indree asked, stretching as they emerged from the invocation hall into the fading sunlight.

They'd pulled the last student they'd interviewed from class within.

Tane glanced at the list. "Randolf Cranst. Not one of our better prospects." They'd gone through the most likely names hours ago. "An average student, no standout subject that looks particularly suspicious. He missed two classes last week and was absent yesterday, but he's far from alone there. Not registered as immediate family of any members of the Guard, but he shares a surname with one. Dedric Cranst. Could be cousins, if we're lucky."

Kadka yawned wide. "Maybe we break, yes? Eat something?" She hadn't bothered to hide her boredom for the past few hours. Showing her teeth had helped get certain students talking a little bit faster, but otherwise there wasn't much for her to do—especially not under the watchful eye of a bluecap.

"We're almost through the list," said Tane. "Only a few names left."

"Then we keep at it," said Indree. "Where do we find Cranst?"

"No classes just now, it looks like," said Tane. "He has a room in the dormitories."

"Come on, then." Indree headed across the campus center toward the northeast corner, where the dormitories were located.

The campus wasn't as quiet as it had been the day before, but it wasn't near as lively as Tane remembered either. The guards were still checking badges at doors, and beyond that, there was a new presence that he hadn't expected: the Mageblades, elite guardians of the Protectorate. A handful of them were scattered around campus at strategic points, imposing in brass cuirasses engraved with the Protectorate's gryphon over blue and white uniforms. Glyph-etched sabers and dual ancryst pistols hung at their sides.

Trained to wield magic in combat in a way few mages could, the Mageblades were utterly loyal to the Protector of the Realm, and their abilities were legendary. By reputation, they could best anyone with spell or sword, and make impossible shots with their ancryst guns, guiding the ball's path with magical fields. Tane had known that Lady Abena was concerned about what had happened in the workshop, but even so he hadn't expected such a strong gesture. She hadn't sent many, but even one would have been a powerful deterrent against anyone looking to cause more trouble. Passing by a towering ogren in cuirass and uniform at the entrance to the dormitories, Tane felt oddly compelled to avoid eye-contact, as if the Mageblade might see everything he was hiding at a single glance.

Cranst shared a room on the third floor with another student—a dwarf by the name of Heln Stonehand. It was Stonehand who answered the door when Indree knocked, and only by a crack, just enough to peek through. Tane could only tell it wasn't Cranst by height. "Yes?"

Indree showed him her badge. "Constable Inspector Indree Lovial. I'm looking for Randolf Cranst."

Stonehand sighed, and opened the door wider, revealing a wide-nosed dwarven face half-hidden by a bushy auburn beard. "What did he do?" His eyes fell on Kadka, and widened. "Oh."

Tane raised an eyebrow. "Oh what? You think he did something to Kadka?"

"I thought… she's orcish, and Rand… he's been talking a lot about magical superiority lately. Some people, they take a first year magical history class and suddenly every conversation ends with 'maybe the Mage Emperor wasn't so wrong'." Stonehand turned to Kadka once more, obviously concerned. "He didn't try to hurt you, did he?"

"Don't know," said Kadka. "That is why we come. To find out."

Indree peered over Stonehand's head into the room. "He's not here, I gather." It was fairly obvious: the room was just large enough to fit a bed and desk on each side, all of it visible from the door.

"No. He hasn't been sleeping here much the last few weeks." Stonehand stepped aside. "You can look through his things if you want. Honestly, the way he's been talking, I've been wondering if I should tell someone."

Indree was inside before he finished inviting her. "Which side is his?"

"There." Stonehand pointed to the right side of the room.

Indree set to work immediately, opening the top drawer of Cranst's desk and sifting through papers and trinkets. Tane followed her in; Kadka closed the door behind and leaned back against it, guarding against interruption.

Tane picked up a small pamphlet from the top of the desk, clearly printed on some basement press. *Magic for the Magical* was the slogan stamped crookedly along the top, followed by a screed about the superiority of mages. The Mage Emperor's staff and crown was emblazoned in the middle of the page. "Look at this." He showed it to Indree.

He recognized the glint in her eye—the same one he'd seen there a hundred times before, when the solution to a problem was coming clear. But aloud, all she said was, "It could be something. But not by itself." She started digging through the next drawer down.

Tane sat on the edge of the bed and looked up at Stonehand. "Any idea where he's been, if not here?"

The dwarf shrugged. "He stays with his cousin sometimes. In Greenstone I think, not far from the Conservatory off Rosepetal Park." Rosepetal Park sat on the edge of the Citadel Court at the center of Thaless, but it was a large park, and the Conservatory of Magical Beasts was situated at the far southern end, bordering on a much less affluent district—better for animal noises to wake some poor miner in the night than the Rhienni ambassador. "If you want me to guess… what if he found some like-minded people? Maybe having some sort of meetings? That could get dangerous."

"His cousin," said Tane. "Is that Dedric Cranst? From the University Guard?"

"That's him."

Again Tane caught Indree's eye, and saw the same understanding there. This was easily the best lead they'd found all day.

But there was something strange about it, too. "Would you call Randolf a gifted student?" Tane asked. "Did he have any particular insight into magical theory?"

Stonehand looked at him incredulously. "Rand? No, not at all. He's studying invocation, but he's average at best. I've had to help him with some pretty basic concepts."

The records said much the same—sometimes tests and grades didn't tell the entire story, but in this case it seemed they did. *So how did he find a loophole in the portal wards that I can't see?*

Indree was on the last desk drawer now, and she'd only had it open a moment when she frowned and drew out a crumpled piece of paper.

"Tane." She showed it to him.

A schedule of student and faculty hours in the primary artifice workshop.

"Well that's *definitely* something," said Tane.

"The cousin," said Indree. "Is he on campus now?"

Tane looked over the guard roster. "He should be on duty."

Indree's eyes went unfocused a moment, and then, "I've sent to Dean Greymond. She'll have him waiting for us in her office. Come on."

When they were outside, away from Stonehand's ears, Kadka said, "This is him, you think?"

"It makes sense," said Tane. "Lady Abena is supposed to share the airship designs with the Continent as a gesture of goodwill. That might look like a sign of weakness, if you were interested in magical superiority. He might have gone after the plans in the hopes of finding a way to sabotage tomorrow's launch."

Indree was several steps ahead, and walking fast. "He could also just be one of a hundred harmless idiots who thinks a first-year class was enough to show him how the whole world works. What we need to know is whether he could have taken his cousin's badge. Hurry up."

Greymond's door, as usual, swung open before they knocked. She was waiting behind her desk. In a chair at the side of the room sat Dedric Cranst, a broad-shouldered human man with thinning brown hair, dressed in a University Guard uniform. He looked up nervously as they entered.

"Inspector Lovial," said Greymond, and gestured at the guardsman. "As requested."

"What is all this?" Cranst asked.

"Mister Cranst, I won't waste time," said Indree. "Your cousin is Randolf Cranst, correct?"

"Y—yes, Inspector."

"Did he stay at your home the night before last?" It was new, seeing Indree like this—every inch the no-nonsense constable.

"Yes he did. He does sometimes, when his roommate is… you know, with someone. But what—"

"Would he have been able to take your badge between midnight and two o'clock the night before last, and again just after noon yesterday?"

"What? No, he wouldn't do that." Dedric's eyes widened. "Wait, those times… you don't think he—"

"Answer the question, Mister Cranst. Not whether you think he would or would not, but whether he had access to the badge."

"I… I suppose while I was sleeping. And I wasn't on duty yesterday. I was out in the afternoon. Listen, Rand is a bit hot-headed, but he would *never*… what happened to that poor girl, that wasn't him."

"Do you know where your cousin is right now?"

"I don't… I haven't seen him today."

Indree was almost certainly using a truth-spell herself, but even so she glanced at Greymond, who gave her a slight nod. Tane didn't raise an objection—it didn't sound to him like the man was lying, and two divinations were probably enough.

"Then we're done here," Indree said. "Dean Greymond, please make certain that he is kept under watch until the constables arrive to take over. I don't want him getting word to his cousin." She didn't hesitate a moment before heading back out the door. Tane and Kadka hurried after.

"So this Cranst *is* mage we fought." Kadka easily matched Indree's pace, leaving Tane several steps behind.

"Looks like." Indree didn't break stride.

"How do we find him now?" Kadka asked.

"We have cause to justify a divination focus," Indree said. "We should be able to pull something from his room." She cursed under her breath. "I've already sent to my superiors. They're arranging a warrant, but we can't afford to spend long digging around for hairs right now. If he tries to contact his cousin he'll realize something is wrong, and mask himself from seeking spells."

"Will these do?" Tane asked. He fished around in his pocket and then thrust his hand between the two women. A few tangled strands of brown hair sat in his open palm.

Indree stopped mid-stride to look down at the hairs, and then back to Tane, frowning. "Where did you…"

"His pillow, when we were in his room. I had a feeling."

"Tane, that's against the law. We didn't have cause or warrant."

He shrugged. "I'm no bluecap. *You* didn't break any rules."

"You're going to get yourself arrested one day. I hope you don't expect me to get you out of it." And then Indree's mouth tugged up at the corner, just a bit, and she snatched the hairs from his hand. "Come on. We're wasting time."

CHAPTER ELEVEN

―――――

"*ANY SIGN OF* Cranst?" Dean Greymond's voice, accompanied by a sudden pressure in his ears. She sounded nervous. As the University's liason to the investigation, she'd insisted Tane keep her informed—she was more familiar with him than with Indree, which made the sending easier.

"We're just off the discs in Porthaven," Tane sent back through the open link. "He's still masked, but Indree thinks we're getting closer."

Indree's seeking spell had found a bearing on Cranst, but his Astral signature was blurred. A cursory masking—probably not a sign that he knew they were coming—but enough that even the divination focus couldn't give her more than a broad sense of his location until they were closer. She'd led them to Porthaven, and from there toward the north side of the harbor. Wherever they were going, it wasn't terribly far from the airship's drydock. The narrow streets were falling into shadow as the sun set overhead. It reminded Tane a little bit too much of the night before. He half-expected a burst of spellfire from the rooftops at any moment.

Indree led them briskly through the streets and alleys, Cranst's hair clutched tight in one hand and her ancryst pistol in the other. He'd been taken aback when she'd drawn it from beneath her coat—it was still hard to look at her and see a bluecap.

"How did you end up here, Ree?"

"Indree," she corrected reflexively.

"Sorry. Indree. But really, why this? You were at the top of your class. You could be drafting spells for any of the manufacturing firms in Thaless for more money in a day than a constable makes in a month."

Indree glanced over her shoulder, and something flickered across her eyes. "Really? You're asking now?"

Tane shrugged. "It just… this isn't something you ever talked about." He didn't really expect an answer, but it was a distraction from his growing unease.

"You don't know me very well anymore, Tane." She was silent a moment, and then she surprised him. "I wasn't angry when I learned the truth about you, you know. I already knew about your parents, and after I read your dissertation, I… well, I suppose I *was* angry. But not the way everyone else was. I just wanted to understand. I wanted you to explain.

She didn't look back again, just kept talking as she led the way. "I didn't give up, after you disappeared. Everyone said you'd just run away. Even Allaea…" Her voice failed her, for just an instant. "Even she said you weren't coming back. She always liked you, but she knew. Me, I didn't think you could do something like that. I thought something had happened to you. Someone had heard about the way you fooled the University and decided to punish you for it. It kept me awake at night.

"So I tried to find you. I cast seeking spells, but you were masked, which only scared me more. Someone was trying to keep you from me. I tried a focus, a hair you left in my bed, but even then you were too well hidden. The focus was just enough to get me a slight feeling every few days when the masking started to fade, before a new one went up. Not enough to find you. But I did my research.

Looked into every seeking and masking spell I could find, tracked the times when the mask seemed to weaken. I kept trying. Every day, for weeks. And then one day there was a gap. I suppose they—you—thought no one would be looking by then. But I was.

"It didn't last very long, but it led me to Porthaven. I had an area. And every day I went back there, looking for some sign. Until one day I saw you, across the street, strolling through the fish market." Her fist clenched tighter around the strands of Cranst's hair. "You weren't in trouble. No one had taken you away. You were just... there.

"It was just like Allaea said. She... she was always better at seeing things like that. I should have given up on you as soon as you left. And after that, I did." Still she didn't look at him, but she squared her shoulders and raised her chin a little higher. "But I learned that I was good at that kind of divination. The kind the constabulary specializes in. And there are always people in this city in real trouble, people with families and friends who are just as scared and worried as I was. People who need help. So I decided to help."

Tane hung his head. "I'm so sorry, Indree. I didn't mean to... I thought I was helping you. You would have been expelled too, if they'd thought you were part of it." *I should have known she wouldn't quit. When has she ever?*

"I don't care," Indree said flatly. "I'm not looking for an apology, and I'm long past expecting to understand. I just wanted you to hear what it was like, not knowing. So if anyone else"—she glanced at Kadka, there—"is stupid enough to get close to you, maybe you don't put them through that."

Kadka didn't react at all to the rather pointed hint— she appeared to be listening to something else entirely. And Tane recognized the look on her face.

"There's someone following us again, isn't there?" He touched his watch case nervously, and then reached into his trouser pockets to check the charms there, better organized than the last time—darkness on the right and charmglobe on the left, loaded and wound with a flash charm inside.

"Many someones," said Kadka. "I think we are surrounded."

Indree frowned. "No, I…" Her eyes glazed a moment, and then, "Spellfire, I was concentrating so much on Cranst, I didn't think… She's right. I can sense maybe a dozen, all around us. His cousin must have warned him. It's a trap, and I led us right into it."

Kadka had a knife in her hand now, and she bared her teeth. "Not over yet."

"You're right." Indree raised her pistol and drew her baton from beneath her coat. Again, a cloud passed across her eyes. "I've notified Stooketon Yard. They're tracking my location, and there were already men on the way to help take Cranst in. We only need to hold until they get here."

"Come then," said Kadka. "Why wait to fight where they want?" She sprinted ahead. Tane exchanged a look with Indree; she raised her shoulders slightly, and followed Kadka.

A man in a black coat darted from an alley ahead to cut Kadka off. She didn't even slow, just lowered her shoulder and hit him full on. He went down. She didn't.

Tane heard the sound of the *lingua* coming from somewhere deeper in, and he recognized the words. Spellfire. "Kadka!" He lunged ahead, grabbed her arm, and pulled her back. A gout of silver flame poured from the shadowed mouth of the alley, barely missing her. Tane looked back, but there were already men emerging along the street behind.

"Stop!" Indree pointed her pistol at a second black-clothed man emerging from the alley ahead—the one who had cast the spellfire, Tane guessed. "By the authority of Stooketon Yard, I demand you let us pass!"

More came after him, from the side-streets ahead and behind, all dressed in black. Men and women, most human, but there were others too: a pair of dwarves, an elf, a kobold, a goblin, a gnome. Very soon the street was blocked by a half-dozen in either direction. A few of them brandished weapons, and one woman wore an ancryst pistol at her hip, but it was the unarmed ones Tane found most worrisome. By the extremist literature he'd found in Cranst's room, he had a feeling that most of them would be mages. Magic users tended to assume their spells were better than any weapon, and they rarely carried ancryst pistols or the like unless extensively trained—their own magic would throw their shots off course.

The man Indree was aiming at laughed. "Let you pass? You're in no position to make demands. Three of you, and two with no magic. You think an orc"—he spat the word with disgust—"can best a mage?" He looked to Tane, ignoring Indree's pistol. "You shouldn't have come after me, Carver. You're out of your depth."

"Cranst." It had to be. He was dressed in a black top-coat over dark clothes, but he hadn't bothered with the mask. There was a certain resemblance to Dedric, though Randolf was younger, with a stronger jaw and a full head of brown hair.

Pressure in his ears, and then Greymond's voice: "Mister Carver, have you—"

"Not now!"

She must have recognized the urgency in his words, because the pressure abated immediately.

"I told you to let the scrollcaster be," Cranst said. "If you had, maybe less people would have gotten hurt. But I had to deal with it."

Bastian. Tane glanced at Kadka, and saw the same realization on her face. His fingers wrapped around the charm in his right pocket. It was the only one worth using at this close a range. Anything else would affect Indree and Kadka too.

Kadka snarled at Cranst. "Enough talk. You want us dead, come try."

"Gladly," Cranst answered with a sour smile. "One less orc in the world." He started to utter words in the *lingua*.

One advantage to pre-cast spells: they were much faster than speaking the words in the moment. "Get ready to move," Tane whispered to Indree and Kadka. They were going to have to do the rest—he wasn't going to be much use in a moment.

He drew his hand from his pocket, crushed the charm's seal, and threw the little roll of paper to the ground at his feet.

The street went black.

CHAPTER TWELVE

———

KADKA'S EYES ADJUSTED almost instantly to the sudden darkness, casting the world in washed-out shades of pale color. Amid cries of alarm and confusion, she threw herself to the side. Carver and Indree did the same.

Silver spellfire roared across the space where they'd been standing.

The strange thing was, the flames didn't light the darkness at all. Kadka could see them clearly, but the light didn't *go* anywhere. The magelights along the side of the street were the same: globes of isolated silver-blue that illuminated only themselves. And yet the darkness wasn't absolute—something filtered in from outside, like a sliver of starlight peeking through on a clouded night. Whatever charm Carver had worked, it seemed to stop magical illumination in its tracks, while allowing just enough natural light for those blessed with keen night eyes. Even under these circumstances, it was a wonder to see, like so many things in this city that so few seemed to notice.

Other voices were already starting to chant in the strange language of magic that Carver called *lingua*. A quick sweep told Kadka that most of them were utterly blind in the dark, save for two dwarves, a goblin, and an elf—those four moved like they could still see.

Kadka leapt for one of the dwarves, a woman chanting nonsense magical words. The ones who could see were the danger now, and spellcasters above the rest. A fist to the throat cut the spell off mid-cast, just like Carver had said. *Blind them, distract them, shut them up*. That was the gist of the advice he'd given her for fighting mages, and he'd provided the darkness already—it was only fair she do her part.

The goblin came at her next, and to her disappointment he didn't try a spell, just swiped at her with a knife of his own. She grabbed his wrist, spun, and heaved, lifting him over her shoulder and slamming him down on the ground.

Indree's half-elven eyes must have been keen enough to pierce the dark too, because she aimed her pistol at the second dwarf. But she didn't shoot. Instead, she spoke a sequence of magic words—quick and practiced, unlike some of their attackers—and from nowhere, bands of translucent silver-blue wrapped around the dwarf's mouth and wrists and ankles. Indree flicked the barrel of her pistol downward and spoke another word, and he was forced to his knees. One of the humans stumbled blindly at her, and she backhanded him across the face with the baton in her other hand. He went down, at least for the moment.

Kadka was impressed, and not just by the spell. The woman knew how to take care of herself.

Carver, not so much. Unable to see in the dark, he'd pressed himself to the ground just ahead, trying to stay out of the way, but a kobold man was only a few steps from tripping over him. Kadka lifted the gasping dwarven woman by the collar and heaved her at the kobold. Both fell in a heap, and Carver scrambled away from the noise. Behind her, Kadka heard the elven man utter the first words of a spell; she whirled and threw her knife in the same motion. The blade bit deep into the elf's shoulder, and a scream of pain signalled his broken concentration.

Someone *else* was muttering the words of a spell, but before Kadka could find him by the sound, Carver's voice interrupted. "Idiot! If you start throwing spellfire without a precise target, you're going to burn each other alive!" The strange words ended abruptly.

She was starting to understand what he'd said about most mages not being trained for battle.

A flicker of movement ahead. Kadka looked up to see Cranst sprinting away down the street. Apparently his confidence had only lasted as long as his advantage. She drew another knife and hurled it, but at the same moment a tall human finished speaking a spell, and a barrier of silver-blue energy blossomed from his hands to span the street. Kadka's blade rebounded from the shield, sending silver ripples over its surface. She had another knife in hand before it hit the ground, but the way forward was blocked. Cranst was out of reach.

The goblin was up again, and he'd given up on a fair fight—he was sneaking up on Carver, who had crawled away to huddle against the wall. The goblin raised a blade. No time for Kadka to get there. "Carver, watch out!"

Indree spun toward Carver and aimed her pistol at a spot on the left side of the silver shield, where no one was standing at all. There was a silvery flash from the barrel, and at almost the same moment the shield rippled bright where the ball neared it and banked away. An instant later the goblin man cried out and dropped.

"Not bad!" Kadka said, grinning wide. She *liked* this woman.

Another man staggered past, blind in the dark. He flinched at the sound of her voice, but he couldn't avoid the hilt of her knife against his temple. He collapsed. Normally she might have killed him outright—he'd attacked them first, after all—but there were still questions to ask, and she suspected Indree would object to a slaughter. Better if they could be friends.

Before she could find another target, a wave of silver force struck her in the side, throwing her against hard brick. She hit the wall laughing, even as her arm twisted and her vision blurred. It hurt, but it was *magic*. Nothing she'd ever done before warmed her blood like this. She didn't think she'd ever get tired of it.

She landed on her feet, searching the direction the spell had come from. The dwarven woman had risen to her knees, and she was already casting another spell.

Kadka charged, snarling for effect—people in the city didn't seem to like when she showed her teeth. The dwarf's eyes widened, and she fell back on her hands, scrambling to get out of the way.

She didn't get far.

Kadka's momentum carried her foot hard into the other woman's windpipe, and the dwarf went down, choking and grasping her throat. *Won't be speaking again soon.*

She glanced from side to side, looking for someone else to fight.

And then, suddenly, she was standing in the dim light of the evening once more. Carver's charm was spent.

———

The darkness was gone, but Tane didn't much like what there was to see.

There were still seven of them standing, one holding a shield-spell to cover Cranst's escape. Kadka closed with a gnome who was chanting a spell and backing away too swiftly for his illusory camouflage to keep pace. Indree had stowed her spent pistol; she was speaking in the *lingua* and fending off a big human man with her baton, all while maintaining her shackling spell on a dwarf nearby. That was impressive—most mages couldn't hold more than one spell and still do much else. A wave of force erupted from her hand, hurling the man she'd been fighting against the magical shield blocking the street. The shield flickered under the force of her spell, but held; the man fell to the ground on his hands and knees.

The ladies were holding their own, but they couldn't last against so many. *If just one mage gets a spell off...* But it wasn't a spell that spurred Tane into motion. As Indree turned to face the other attackers, a human woman put her back against the shield and took aim with an ancryst pistol. From there, the magical force of the barrier wouldn't interfere with the shot—it would send it right into Indree's back.

"Ree!" Tane didn't have time to think, just threw himself forward, yanking the daze-wand from his belt as he moved.

He leapt at the woman with the pistol and jabbed toward her torso, hoping for the best. They collided hard; she caught the wand with one hand, holding the end inches from her chest. The pistol went off in a silver flash. The two of them pitched to the ground in a tangle of limbs.

The woman held the wand tight and battered Tane's head and shoulders with her expended pistol. He gritted his teeth and pushed, avoiding the blows as best he could. Then, all at once, he relaxed his arm. She wasn't expecting it. Her grip weakened for an instant, and he shoved again with all his strength. The copper tip of the wand touched her chest, and she went limp. The already cloudy peridot set above the grip was entirely consumed by opaque white, and a crack ran down the center as the last of its structural integrity was utterly consumed by magic.

Tane rolled off the woman, panting. His eyes found Indree. Still on her feet. "Thank the Astra," he breathed.

"Stop where you are!" A new voice from behind. Tane lifted his head to see a dozen uniformed bluecaps approaching from behind, pistols drawn.

Some of the remaining attackers threw down their weapons; others tried to run, but the constables restrained them with shackling spells similar to the one Indree was maintaining on the dwarven man. The human holding the shield bolted down a side-alley, and the shimmering barrier flickered and vanished. Three constables were after him the instant the way was clear.

"About time," Indree said, but she was smiling, and the relief was clear on her face. "Take them to the Yard. We'll want to question them." The constables closed in, binding the prisoners with shackles and brass muzzles to stop the mages from casting.

Kadka pulled Tane to his feet and clapped him on the back. "Carver! Is clever thing, this darkness!"

Indree had released her spell on the dwarf now that he was bound, and she was tapping a small amount of silver powder into her pistol—firing charms didn't carry much force unless enhanced with silver, but the powder was consumed along with the charm, requiring a new load for each shot. "Don't give him all the credit. You must have dropped at least five yourself. That was… impressive."

Kadka bared her teeth in a wide grin. "Is more they were not. And you are not so bad yourself."

"I had spells, and my pistol. You took more of them with a few knives." Indree finished tamping the ancryst ball and charm into the barrel of her gun, and looked up at Tane. "And the charm helped. That *was* quick thinking, Tane. It probably saved our lives." She glanced at the woman he'd dazed, still limp on the ground. "Thank y—" Her eyes widened and she broke off mid-word. One hand dipped into her pocket, and came out with a strand of brown hair. "Cranst! We might still catch him!" And then she was off down the street, with Tane and Kadka sprinting after.

Cranst hadn't gotten far, as it turned out. He was waiting at the end of the road where it met the harbor, just a few blocks south of the airship and its towering scaffolds. He must have known that his ambush had failed—

that there was no escape while Indree was alive and still had a focus on him. A forced rictus of a smile stretched across his face, but Tane saw fear in his eyes. The last faint light of the setting sun glinted off the long knife in his hand.

"Drop the weapon, Cranst." Indree levelled her pistol at him.

"They were supposed to stop you," Cranst said, his voice trembling. "You weren't supposed to come after me."

"Did you kill Allaea?" The pistol shook slightly in Indree's hands, but she kept her voice steady. "Confess, and it will go toward a merciful sentence."

"She wasn't supposed to be there. Another failure. I… I made a mess of it."

"A mess of *what?*" A raw edge crept into Indree's voice as her composure failed. "What did she die for? What were you doing?"

"You… you won't get anything from me!" His voice broke, but he raised his knife in both hands. "I may have failed, but the time of the magical will come again! You can't stop it!"

Tane took a step toward him. "Cranst, don't!"

"For the Mage Emperor!" Cranst screamed, and drove the knife into his chest with both hands.

Tane surged forward as Cranst collapsed to the ground, face first. "Get help! He might—"

"There's no point." Indree approached slowly, staring at the crumpled body. "The blade went through his heart. I can feel him fading from the Astra. He killed her, and he can't even tell me why." With a strangled cry of rage, she aimed a savage kick at Cranst's head. "*Why?*"

Cranst jerked limply at the impact, but he was beyond answering.

Tane wanted to say something, offer some comfort, but he didn't think she'd welcome that from him just then.

Instead, it was Kadka who went to her. She placed a

fur-tufted hand on Indree's shoulder. "You found man who killed her. This is not nothing."

"It's not enough," said Indree. But she didn't pull away.

"He might have something that can tell us more," Tane said, and started to pat down the body, trying to avoid the spreading blood. "Here." A small purse, tucked into an inner pocket of Cranst's coat. Tane emptied it into his palm. A plain iron key and… "A badge?" Not University Guard, though—this wasn't what he'd used to get into the workshop.

A gold crown and staff on a circle of deep purple. The Mage Emperor's sigil.

"Look at this," Tane said, holding it up. "For the wards on his bolthole? Or maybe… all the magical extremist rhetoric, and those others with him… some sort of cult, like Stonehand thought?"

Indree leaned down to look. "It could be. We'll question the others, they might—" She stopped, frowned. "Tane?"

"What?"

"He said something about a scrollcaster." She was glaring at him now, in that terrifying way only she could. "What. Scrollcaster."

"Spellfire, I nearly forgot!" Tane locked eyes with Kadka over Indree's shoulder. "We need to get to Bastian. Now."

CHAPTER THIRTEEN

———

AT THE BOTTOM of the short stairway off the alley, the door to Bastian's workshop stood half-open.

Tane couldn't imagine that was a good sign.

Indree stopped Tane and Kadka with a raised hand, and then waved the constables forward. Four bluecaps followed her in, pistols and batons at the ready—she'd left the others to bring in the prisoners.

Tane glanced at Kadka, who tipped her head toward the door. He shrugged and nodded, and they stepped inside, disregarding Indree's signal.

The bodies were the first thing Tane noticed. Six of them, and none looked to have died very pleasantly. He recognized four as Bastian's "friends", three humans sprawled on the floor and a goblin bent over a worktable with terrible burns across his back. The last two must have been with the intruders, a human and an elf slumped against one another, both in black coats and trousers like Cranst and the rest had worn. At first glance, there was no sign of a little sprite in a green mask and waistcoat.

The room had been thoroughly ransacked. Dark scorch marks marred the walls at various points. Books littered the floor, and the dais beside Bastian's little library had been toppled, the tiny furniture left in pieces. Tables had been shifted and tipped over in what must have been a violent fight for the scrollcaster, and artifacts were scattered everywhere, most of them broken. The charms must have been incinerated with spellfire—only a few remained intact amid drifts of ash and scraps.

Indree gave the two of them an annoyed glance as they entered, but she didn't waste time on reprimands. "We're looking for a brass scrollcaster set with a peridot," she instructed the bluecaps. "It's possible they didn't find it. Cranst made implications, but he didn't say anything outright. Spread out and search." The constables did as she ordered, sifting through the mess. Tane had explained the situation to her on the way—she hadn't been terribly pleased, but she'd been more concerned with retrieving the caster than scolding him, so far.

"How did they get in?" Tane wondered aloud. "There were wards when we came."

"It doesn't matter now," said Indree. "Do either of you have any idea where he might have put the scrollcaster?"

Tane shook his head. "No, I—"

He felt a pressure in his ears, and then Bastian appeared just in front of his face. One moment the space was empty, and the next, a fat little sprite in a masquerade mask hovered in front of him on iridescent wings. Tane took a startled step back. Beside him, Kadka did the same.

"Hello!" Bastian said. "Mister Carver and my dear Kadka, I'm so pleased to see you again. If only it were under better circumstances. I'd intended to contact you shortly, but my detections tell me you've already seen this unspeakable tragedy for yourselves."

"What is it?" Indree demanded. "What are you two looking at?" She waved a hand through the air in front of Tane's face; it passed through Bastian as if he wasn't there.

"You don't see?" Kadka asked. She mimicked Indree's gesture, passing her hand through Bastian's belly. Her eyes widened.

Indree raised an eyebrow. "I don't see anything. A sending?"

Tane nodded. "The contact I told you about. This was his shop."

"Ah, yes, I did detect a number of bluecaps with you," said the illusory Bastian. "How strange this must look to them! I'm afraid they won't see or hear me, nor I them—a shared sending seemed the most efficient way to contact you both, but I haven't any divination foci for your friends. Under any other circumstances I would be very cross with you for leading the authorities to my humble shop, but tonight I can hardly complain!"

"Ask him what happened," Indree said urgently. "We need to know where the scrollcaster is."

"I know. Let me talk to the man." Tane waved Indree away. She scowled at him, but moved to help her men search the wreckage. "What happened here, Bastian?"

"A young man came in with two others. He knew the proper procedures, my secret knock. A pity. I'll have to change it now, and I did rather like the rhythm. Suffice it to say, there was nothing overly suspicious about them, other than a certain nervousness. I suspect now that their leader must have been the masked student we discussed— not masked this time, of course. He would have known how to get in the door."

"Dark hair and eyes, a sharpish jawline?"

"Yes, yes that sounds like the man!"

Cranst. He must have come straight from Bastian's shop to the street where they'd been ambushed. "Go on," said Tane.

"My friends searched them for weapons and found nothing. The young men acted only after our guard was lowered. One of them raised a shield while the others cast spellfire at the warding glyphs around the room. It wasn't terribly swift or skillful, but I must admit, we were wholly unprepared for such a barbaric attack! There is a certain honor among my colleagues, criminal or no. A certain way of doing things. But this... It simply isn't done!" Bastian fluttered his wings in obvious agitation. "They were successful in damaging the wards, in any event, even with the redundancies I had in place. After that, more came. My friends were able to get me out through a passage in the back, at a... rather terrible cost." He hung his head. "But I am afraid I have let you down rather gravely, Mister Carver. These... these *savages* destroyed the scrollcaster you entrusted to me."

"But you still have focus for us," said Kadka. "Why take these when you go, and not caster?"

"I had the scrollcaster on my desk, in plain sight. By the time I gathered my wits, it was already too late to save it. I fled with nothing but my life, I assure you! I have the foci only because I store my collection at a separate location. I do have resources beyond this shop, my dear! One must be ready to relocate quickly, in this business!" Bastian puffed out his chest slightly, as if that was a matter of personal pride.

"There's nothing here," Indree said from across the room. "What does this contact of yours have to say?"

Tane didn't want to answer. She wasn't going to like this, and he couldn't blame her.

Kadka had no such hesitation. "Was Cranst. Scrollcaster is gone. Destroyed."

"Damn it!" Indree slammed a hand down on one of the tables. "If you'd just told me about it sooner—"

"I know!" Tane snapped, and then, after a breath, "I'm not happy about this either. But... you would have taken it, and then we'd never have gotten anything out of Bastian. He was never going to talk to a bluecap."

"Oh dear," the Bastian figment said with a frown, and peered around as if searching for Indree and the others. His eyes passed over them, unseeing. "I hope I haven't gotten you in trouble. It *is* true that I wouldn't have spoken to a constable, if that makes any difference at all."

But Indree couldn't hear him, and by the look on her face it wouldn't have mattered much if she could have. "Maybe that's true," she said, "but it wasn't your decision to make. I know you think you're the smartest man in every room, but… Spellfire, Tane, I should take you in for this. Obstructing my investigation."

"If that's what you want to do, I can't stop you," said Tane. "But at least let me get what I can here first. Bastian might still have something we can use."

Indree looked at him for a long moment, prodding her cheek with her tongue. Finally she nodded, and gestured for him to finish.

Tane looked back to Bastian. "Were you able to get anything from the caster before they took it?"

"Not as much as I would like," said Bastian. "But I was able to discern what it was used for last. It may have sent any number of papers first, but the last thing it did was receive."

Tane narrowed his eyes. "What would he have been receiving? Some sort of instructions? From where?"

"If only I could say!" Bastian's voice positively throbbed with lament. "It was taken before I could find anything more!"

"It's… fine, Bastian." He didn't want the little sprite to burst a blood vessel.

"You can be proud, little man," said Kadka. "You try to help, even at high price. Is good thing."

"I did nothing more than my duty to Lady Abena and the Protectorate!" Bastian said, though he looked rather pleased with himself beneath his mask. "I'm only sorry I can't tell you more. But if there is nothing else you need, this attack has left me with a great deal of work to do."

"Go," said Tane. "But if you remember anything else…"

"Of course, Mister Carver! I want nothing more than to see the man who did this brought to justice!" The illusory sprite turned to Kadka. "And my dearest Kadka, my offer is and shall always remain open. You need only contact my friend Issik."

"Need to finish this," Kadka said. "But when is done, who knows?"

"Ah, how you toy with my hopes. A delight, as ever!" Bastian's sending bowed as deep as his round little body could manage. "I wish you both the best of luck!" And then he was gone.

Indree noticed the change right away. "Well?" she said. "You said something about receiving a message."

"He told me the case was last used to receive, not to send," said Tane

"To receive what?"

"That's the question," Tane said. "He didn't know. New instructions, maybe?"

"Means he was working for someone, then, yes?" Kadka said.

"It might," said Indree. "But it could have come from a subordinate, too. One of the people with him tonight. Until we know what was sent, all we can say for certain is that *someone* sent it. It's something to ask our prisoners about, at least."

"So," said Tane, offering his hands for binding, "are you going to throw me in a cell now?"

"I should." Indree sighed and shook her head, and for a brief, startling moment, Tane could have sworn he saw a smile. "You're an arrogant dunce, Tane Carver, but I do believe you meant well. And we still have something to work with. I suppose you can keep your freedom for now."

"That's what I hoped you'd say. Time to do some questioning, then?"

"It's time for *me* to spend a long night questioning the prisoners," said Indree, "and for you to go home. Without arguing. Because you understand that I'm already turning a blind eye to several misdemeanors, and there is no force in the Astra that would convince the Chief Constable to let you into the Yard unshackled."

There wasn't much room to fight her there. "Fine. I suppose I could use some sleep."

"I'll send someone with you, in case Cranst laid any other traps." Indree turned to Kadka. "I don't know that you're any better than Tane, but please, stop him if he tries to do something stupid like sneak into Stooketon Yard?"

Kadka grinned. "If plan is too bad… maybe I will stop. Could be fun to watch."

"I shudder to think what the two of you might consider a *good* plan, but I suppose that's the best I'm going to get. Now go. I have to get these bodies back to the Yard." Indree gestured to a pair of constables. "See them home."

Tane turned to leave, hesitated, and looked back. "Indree?"

She raised an eyebrow.

"We'll be back tomorrow. I'm not giving up on this."

Another ghost of a smile. "I didn't think for a moment that you would. Greymond's office, first bell. I'll expect you there."

CHAPTER FOURTEEN

***

GREYMOND SCOWLED AT Tane from behind her desk. "Would you mind telling me why I am only hearing about this scrollcaster now? Is it physically *possible* for you to tell the truth, Mister Carver?"

Indree answered before Tane could. "Some secrecy was necessary to appease his contacts in the black market. I agree that he went too far, but what's done is done."

Tane glanced at her, surprised. She looked all too much like an official representative of Stooketon Yard in her constable's uniform with her blue cap over pinned hair—he hadn't expected her to defend his interference. She ignored him, her gaze fixed on Greymond, but Kadka caught Tane's eye and grinned knowingly.

Greymond hardly looked satisfied, but she moved on. "And the prisoners? Did they give you anything?"

Indree shook her head. "Not very much. I questioned every one of them with truth-spells, and as far as I can tell, they don't know anything. A handful of overly suggestible students, and the rest pulled from various Halls of the Astra." That wasn't surprising. Astralites already worshipped the source of magic as a divine entity—it wouldn't be a huge jump from there to magical superiority. "They responded to pro-magical literature like the pamphlet we found in Cranst's room. Apparently he held regular meetings. Some of them are... rather fanatical, but they weren't told anything about his overarching plans. They didn't have badges like we found on him, either." She indicated Cranst's pouch, lying on Greymond's desk. "Divinations on the badge and key confirmed that they belonged to Cranst, but nothing beyond that."

"Can we assume, then, that the matter is closed? Cranst all but admitted to the murder, by your account, and seems to have been the motivating force behind these lunatics."

Tane shook his head. "I don't think it's that simp—"

Greymond interrupted him with a short phrase in the *lingua*, and her office door swung open.

Chancellor Nieris strode into the room in an extravagant purple coat and frilled crimson cravat. "Thank you, Liana," he said briskly, and held the door for the woman behind him.

She was human, perhaps a few years past forty, with deep brown skin—darker than Indree's, who was of Anjican descent on her human mother's side. Her hair was short, dense black curls trimmed close to the scalp. She wore very fine clothes: a pale blue full-skirted longcoat buttoned in silver, with black boots beneath. Tane knew her instantly, even before Nieris introduced her. The air of authority she carried could only belong to a scion of one of the Great Houses, and only one human house traced its roots back to Estian-occupied Anjica before the Mage War.

"May I introduce Lady Abena Jasani, Protector of the Realm," Nieris said. "Lady Abena, I know you are familiar with Dean Greymond."

Lady Abena nodded her head. "It is always a pleasure, Liana. I appreciate—"

"I was glad to help, Your Ladyship, but the constabulary hasn't needed a great deal of assistance. I've done little enough." Greymond went pale then, realizing too late that she'd interrupted the Lady Protector. "Oh I... I'm sorry, I—"

Lady Abena smiled. "Great diviners are always ahead of their time, they say. I take no offense."

Nieris continued around the room. "This is Constable Inspector Indree Lovial, and I imagine you've heard of Mister Tane Carver." He frowned when he got to Kadka. "And Kadka, formerly of the University Guard. I confess, I'm not certain why she is here."

Kadka returned his gaze steadily. "Helping."

"She *has* been a great help, Lady Abena," Indree said quickly, dipping her head respectfully to the Lady Protector. "Without her, I think last night's ambush would have gone very differently."

"Then I thank you, Kadka," said Lady Abena. "If you have been of use to the investigation, you are welcome here. Or is there a problem, Chancellor Nieris?"

"Of course not. As I said before, Miss Kadka, I was very sorry that I had to..." Nieris trailed off under Kadka's yellow-eyed stare. "Well, in any event, we have important things to discuss."

"Yes," said Lady Abena. "I am very interested to hear about what you have found, Inspector Lovial. Chancellor Nieris assures me that your efforts have been most admirable." She turned to Tane, then; his instinct was to bow, but no one else was, so he just dipped his head low. "And Tane Carver. I have long been interested in meeting you. I read your dissertation, years ago. You raised some very interesting points. Of course, my family saw that I was instructed in magical theory by the finest tutors, but not everyone has that privilege. I would not presume to question my predecessor's decisions, but had I been Protector of the Realm at that time... well, there is no use speculating, is there?"

"No, Your Ladyship, I suppose there isn't." Tane swallowed nervously. Protectors of the Realm were elected in the Senate of Houses, and didn't demand the same subservience as born royalty like the Kaiser of Belgrier or theocrats like the Lord Provost of Estia, but still he felt extremely shabby standing before her in his frayed waistcoat. "I'm… glad you found my work interesting, at least." That actually did mean something, coming from her. There were few in the Protectorate's upper ranks who would better understand what he'd been trying to say.

Abena Jasani, like every Protector of the Realm before her, lacked any magic of her own.

No mage could hold Audland's highest office. It was one of the nation's founding principles, to signify that although the Protectorate was founded as a haven for the magical, they did not hold those born with magecraft to be superior to those without. And perhaps more importantly, to prove to the nations of the Continent that they didn't need to fear another Mage Emperor. It made for a strange political reality that in a country so reliant on magic, a senate of houses made wealthy and powerful by magecraft was forced to select a leader from those born without the gift. Less affluent families prayed to the Astra for their children to be mages; in the great houses, the magicless were groomed all their lives for the possibility that they might one day govern the nation. And unique among the highest positions in Audland, Lord and Lady Protectors were almost never elvish, because the elvish were almost never magicless.

Lady Abena smiled. "Perhaps one day, after I have seen my airship into the sky, we can speak more about what you wrote." She looked back to Indree. "But for now, I must know what your investigation has uncovered. Please, Constable Inspector."

Indree summarized the investigation up to the events of the previous night, going so far as to credit Tane and Kadka's assistance as indispensable. Tane wasn't sure if she really meant it or if she was just trying to make the story sound better for Lady Abena, but it was nice to hear either way.

"You see, Lady Abena?" Nieris said. "The matter is dealt with, as I promised. Cranst was behind the murder, and his little cult won't be a problem any longer."

"I'm sorry, Chancellor Nieris, but I'm not so certain," said Indree. "There are still things we don't know. Cranst shouldn't have been able to bypass the portal wards on campus to begin with."

Nieris waved a dismissive hand. "We will look into that, of course, but for now the wards have been tightened and the threat is gone. What matters is that the airship launch can proceed safely."

Indree frowned. "I don't—"

"You understand, Inspector," Nieris said firmly, "that it would not reflect well on anyone if the ceremony were to be put off now. You have done a great deal to assure that does not happen. On behalf of the University, I thank you. The Chief Constable will certainly be hearing from me about your work here."

"You... you have to be joking! Tane sputtered. "You *can't* be that arrogant." He could have screamed. *The same as it always goes. Reputations to uphold. It wouldn't do to announce that the University's mages can make mistakes.*

Nieris gave Tane a look that could have frozen over the Audish Channel. "You are out of line, Mister Carver."

"Out of line? A man opened a portal inside your supposedly unbreakable wards and *murdered* a student! My friend!" Everyone was looking at him now, but he didn't stop. "Cranst didn't break those wards alone. He wasn't close to capable of that. We know he was receiving messages from someone, and we don't know *who*." Tane snatched up the pouch from Greymond's desk, emptied the badge and key into his hand, and lifted them for all to see. "A badge like this implies an organization, and we don't know that we've caught them all. There is still a very real chance someone out there has one like it, which means they have access to wherever Cranst was hiding. And probably to anything he sent out of the artifice workshop. If they're planning to sabotage the airship, they might well have the plans they need to do it. You're a fool if you ignore that!"

"Tane!" Dean Greymond looked absolutely mortified, and she glanced nervously at the Lady Protector.

Which reminded Tane where the true power lay here. He spun to face Lady Abena. "Your Ladyship, please. You have to postpone this until we know more."

"I apologize for this inexcusable outburst, Lady Abena," Nieris said hastily. "Mister Carver, that is more than enough. You will remove yourself immediately, or I will have you removed."

Kadka stepped in front of Tane, her thick jaw set stubbornly. "No. We stay. Carver is right. You should listen."

Tane pushed past her. "This is between me and the chancellor, Kadka." He gave her a pointed look, tried to tell her with his eyes what he couldn't say aloud. *Stay out of this. You don't have to go down with me.* But she only stared at the chancellor, unflinching.

Nieris rubbed his temples. "Have you both taken leave of your senses? I can have the Guard—"

Lady Abena held up one hand. "That will not be necessary, Talain," she said, and then to Tane, "I admire your conviction, Mister Carver, and I share your concerns."

"Then you'll postpone?"

She shook her head. "I truly wish that I could, but the ceremony must go forward. Too much depends on it. You must understand: we are a small nation, and the larger ones across the Channel have no love of us or our magic. Smaller conflicts have been piling on one another for years, and I fear they will soon lead to a war we cannot afford. My airships and the promise they represent are, I believe, the best hope of a lasting peace. Perhaps even a chance to better the lives of our magical cousins on the Continent. But if the dignitaries attending tonight sense that something is awry with the launch, that opportunity could be lost. A hint of doubt is all it would take."

That was a hard thing to argue against. For centuries now, the Protectorate hadn't gone more than thirty years at a time absent some conflict with the nations that bordered the Audish Channel on the Calenean side. Each had reacted to the Mage War differently, but they were all wary of magic to some degree. In Estia, the remnant of the old empire had turned to a religious dogma that called magecraft a corruption of the soul—though they somehow justified ancryst engines to keep their naval presence strong. In Belgrier, they saw the magical as a danger, segregating them into ghettos and workhouses. Even in Rhien, the least severe of the three, those with magic in their blood were allowed to live as citizens only under constant government oversight. Lady Abena had long preached improved ties of trade and travel and diplomacy as the most practical solution to the problem, even before she had been named Protector of the Realm.

"So what, then?" Tane said. "We just... close our eyes and hope nothing goes wrong?"

"No," said Lady Abena. "We ensure it does not. My Mageblades will secure the launch site itself, and there are few who would dare to stand against them, as I'm sure you know." She looked to Indree. "But I would also ask that Stooketon Yard send men to patrol the whole of Porthaven, and conduct a full search of the area for any remaining saboteurs before the ceremony begins this evening. And during the event, perhaps a number of constables in dress attire among the guests?"

Indree nodded. "Of course, Your Ladyship. I will see it done. Cranst ambushed us not far from the airship, and it seems likely he would have kept his hiding place near there. We may yet end this before the ceremony starts. If not, I will personally coordinate a covert detail."

"Your dedication speaks highly of you, Constable Inspector," said Lady Abena. "And Mister Carver, Miss Kadka: whatever your reservations, I ask that you help however you can. I know you have both been invaluable to this investigation. The Protectorate needs you now."

It was almost exactly what Tane had told Bastian the day before, but it was hard to see it as the same sort of cheap trick when it came from the Protector of the Realm herself. "I... I'll do my best, Your Ladyship."

Kadka inclined her head. "Too far in to not go farther. I want to see what end looks like."

"Thank you." Lady Abena spread her hands in a wide gesture. "All of you, for everything you have done and the work to come. Now, I believe it would be best not to delay any longer."

Tane left with Indree and Kadka, doing his best to pretend he didn't notice Greymond and Nieris watching him with disapproving eyes. *I suppose this isn't going to leave me as well positioned with the University as I'd hoped.* But it had needed saying, and no one else would have. The only thing he regretted was dragging Kadka into it.

When they were outside, Indree turned to him. "Tane? I'm going to need that badge and key."

He still had Cranst's empty pouch clutched in one hand, the key and badge in the other. He looked down at them, and hesitated. "Doesn't it seem too easy to assume Cranst's bolthole was in Porthaven? They obviously knew we were coming. Why lead us right to the place they're trying to hide?"

"Besides the fact that they thought we'd be dead?" But Indree didn't sound very certain. "I... don't entirely disagree, Tane. But I'm acting under request from the Lady Protector now. This is the best lead we have. We can't ignore it for a hunch. Even if we don't find anything, a heavy constabulary presence in Porthaven might discourage any attempts to sabotage the airship." She prodded her cheek with her tongue a moment, and then, "But I don't need you two patrolling the docks. If you come up with something better and decide to follow it up, I don't see any harm in that. As long as you don't find some way to cause a diplomatic incident at the launch ceremony."

"No promises," said Tane with a slight smile.

"You were never much for keeping them anyway," Indree said. "I do need the badge and key, though. I can't let you keep important evidence. We'll need them if we do find his hiding place."

Tane stowed the contents of his hand in Cranst's pouch, and handed it over.

"Good luck," said Indree. "And Tane... be careful." She turned to Kadka. "Don't let him get himself killed." Before either one of them could answer, she walked briskly away.

After a moment, Kadka said, "She will not be happy when she finds you kept key and badge."

Tane rubbed his neck sheepishly. "You noticed?"

"I guessed." Kadka grinned as he plucked the key and badge from his sleeve. "What does she have?"

"A silver stave and a spare key to my office."

"So she can unlock door when she comes later to put you in cell. This is thoughtful of you."

"I'm nothing if not considerate." Tane flipped the badge into the air and caught it, glancing at the glyphs on the back side. "She's not going to find a place to use this in Porthaven. I still might."

"Where?"

Tane looked away. "Kadka... maybe you shouldn't come. It's bad enough that I lost you your position with the Guard, but now Nieris is angry with me. With both of us, after you backed me in there. Which you shouldn't have done. Making an enemy of the chancellor could make things very difficult for you in Thaless. It's probably best if you aren't seen with me anymore."

Kadka laughed. "I am not afraid of skinny elf man with all his frills. If you go alone, how do I earn my part of pay?"

"You earned it three saving my lifes ago. I'll give you your share. You don't have to—"

"Carver. Stop. Like I say to your Lady Protector: I

come too far now to not see end. Tell me where we go."

"Spellfire, don't be stubborn about this. I'm trying to help you!"

"Want to help? Let me say what is best for me."

Tane threw up his hands. "Fine! But when things get bad, don't say I didn't warn you."

She just grinned that sharp-toothed grin. "Because is so good, this far?"

Tane tried to hold his glare, but a snorted laugh forced its way out of his nose. "Fair point."

"So. Where to look?"

"I'm… still working on that part," he admitted grudgingly. "We *saw* the room he came from through that portal in the workshop. There might have been some clue there."

"Was blurry. Couldn't see much."

"I know," said Tane. "But… there had to be *something*."

"There was sound," Kadka said.

"Probably just an instability in the portal." He frowned. "Except… we heard it twice. If it was just random sounds pulled through the Astra, would we have heard the same noise twice?"

"I still say it sounds like *tunvok* howling."

"Right." She'd mentioned that before, but he hadn't paid it much mind at the time. "Some sort of animal, you said. What *is* it, exactly?"

"Is like… wolf, you would say. But bigger. Howl brings cold. In Sverna, they are tamed sometimes, to ride."

"Wait… orcish wolf-riders are *real?* Spellfire, I thought that was a story."

Kadka shrugged. "Is real. *Tunvokovir*, they are called."

"Still, that howl had to have come through an instability from Sverna. Where else would you be able to hear…" Tane's eyes widened, and he grabbed her by the shoulders. "Kadka! That's it!"

She grinned broadly, caught up in his enthusiasm. "What is it?"

"Dedric Cranst said his house was near the Conservatory of Magical Beasts! If there are any of these *tunvok* in Thaless, that's exactly where they'd be!"

CHAPTER FIFTEEN

———

"SHE'S JUST DOWN here," the sprite woman said, fluttering down the cobbled paths of the Conservatory. The Head Keeper on duty, Selene Meadowgrass had taken it upon herself to personally assist Tane and Kadka after he'd dropped the Lady Protector's name. She wore exactly the uniform Tane would have imagined an animal-keeper to wear, but in miniature: a khaki coat with a great many pockets, matching trousers, and a wide-brimmed hat over her brown hair. "I should be able to get her to howl for you—we're working on those commands. I'm surprised she hasn't started on her own, to be honest. Some days it seems like she'll never stop."

"Well, we appreciate the help," Tane said, but he was only half-listening. He hadn't visited the Conservatory since he was a boy, and the animals were both incredible and distracting.

Dozens of large fenced habitats lined the path, the smallest of them easily ten times the size of his little office in Porthaven. Magically warded and spelled to mimic environments from deserts to plains to frozen snowdrifts, each housed a beast directly out of ancient legend. To his left, in the forested unicorn habitat, one of the majestic equine creatures bent over a little stream, its spiral horn glimmering with a hundred colors in the afternoon sun. Tane found it hard to look away.

Kadka stared wide-eyed at the right-hand enclosure, a large desert-like environment with sandstone caves all along one side. Inside, a massive lion-headed manticore with bat-like wings and a scorpion tail padded back and forth over arid ground, watching them pass. The enclosure was fully caged, with iron bars overhead. "All these animals live in wild? How do I not hear more of them?"

"There aren't many left." There was just a hint of anger in Selene's voice. "Hunted down for one magical property or another, or just out of fear. Driven from their natural habitats as cities expand here and on the Continent. No one wants a chimera for a neighbor, even if the chimera was there first. Most of the animals we keep here are nearly extinct. The Conservatory's primary purpose is to protect the ones that are left."

They'd moved past the manticore, but Kadka was still looking back, craning her head over her shoulder. "Why do they stay? That one could break bars, if he tried."

"I've trained them too well for that," Selene said with a smile, and Tane believed her. Sprites had a natural affinity for animals. They couldn't actually control beasts, like some people believed, but they could commune with them. "But you aren't wrong. A full-grown manticore could break out of just about any housing we could make. The fences and cages are for show, more than anything. They make people feel safer. It's the wards that really keep them from escaping."

"You have dragons?" Kadka peered around with interest.

Selene shook her head. "Just a wyvern, but he's a bit of a runt. Not much larger than a big dog. True dragons… if they ever existed at all, no one has seen one for centuries."

Tane laughed at Kadka's disappointed pout. "What, unicorns and manticores aren't good enough?"

She grinned. "They are good. Dragon would be better."

"Here we are," said Selene, pointing ahead to an enclosure on the left side of the path. "Olka, our Svernan ice wolf. We've only had her two weeks or so. She's still learning not to keep people up at all hours, but her training is coming along."

"Can't use spell to keep her quiet?" Kadka asked.

"The people who live nearby suggest it every time we get a new addition, but we need to be able to hear when the animals are in distress," said Selene. "For the most part, our residents are trained well enough that it isn't a problem. It just takes time." She landed on an eye-level perch designed for people of her size along the side of the fence, and waved them closer.

The huge enclosure had been made to mimic the Svernan climate, all icy tundra and snowy crust. The ice wolf—or *tunvok*, according to Kadka—padded to the fence as they drew near, her paws crunching against the frozen ground. She looked much as Kadka had described: a massive wolf the size of a horse, with a strange undercoat of pale blue beneath white fur. Her hackles were raised, and her grey-blue eyes traced every movement. Where she breathed, a coat of frost formed on the iron fence.

She growled, and Tane retreated a step, keeping his distance.

"Don't take it personally," Selene said. "She's not very friendly to anyone just yet."

"Maybe never," said Kadka. "Is not easy, taming *tunvok*." She leaned close. The wolf snapped her teeth between the bars, then danced back, confused, when the wards repelled her muzzle. Kadka frowned, but didn't flinch. "Has spirit. She will never be happy here. Is big enough, and looks like home, but still cage."

"It isn't ideal," admitted Selene. "We usually only take animals in when they can't survive safely in their natural habitat, but Olka's situation was... complicated. She'd crossed into northern Rhien from the Svernan border, and she was causing problems for some of the smaller villages there. Killing livestock, freezing crops with her howl. They were scared to get close, so the Rhienni ambassador asked the Conservatory for help. We're still trying to make contact with someone in Sverna about sending her home, and the Rhienni would have killed her if she stayed near the border, so here she is. Where she ends up depends on the diplomats now, but I don't think she's a very high priority."

"Well, she might be the solution to a problem that the Lady Protector wants solved very badly," said Tane. "That could help. Now, I hate to annoy your neighbors, but can we hear her?"

"Of course," said Selene. "Assuming she's in the mood to cooperate." She locked eyes with Olka, and the wolf tilted her head as if listening.

And then Olka raised her muzzle to the sky and let out a long howl.

The sound of it sent a circle of frost racing across the enclosure, expanding rapidly until it reached the fence, coating black iron bars in white rime. The air crackled loudly with the sound of sudden, intense cold; the already frozen ground groaned and split open in places. Even outside the wards, protected from the immediate effect, Tane felt a chill raise gooseflesh across his body.

"That's it," he said. "That's the sound." It was the same as what he'd heard in the workshop, there was no doubting that. "You said you've had complaints. That must give you a sense of how far people can hear her from."

"Just the upper streets of Greenstone, south of here. It's all Rosepetal Park for a ways in the other directions. If anyone hears her from that far, they haven't complained."

"Good. That gives us a place to start looking. I just have one more favor to ask: can you have her howl one more time in about fifteen minutes?"

Selene raised an eyebrow. "I suppose, but why?"

"I want to get an idea of how it sounds from where we're looking," said Tane. "That should give us enough time to get there."

"It shouldn't be a problem."

"Thank you, Selene. You've been a great help."

Selene waved a dismissive hand. "If it's for Lady Abena, I'm glad to do it. Whatever you're looking for, I hope you find it."

Not quite fifteen minutes later, Tane and Kadka arrived at Dedric Cranst's house in northern Greenstone. The squat brick building was divided into four separate homes, and there were more just like it on both sides and on down the street. Each home had its own cramped yard at the back, fenced off from the others and accessible through narrow side alleys. This was the better end of Greenstone, though it was still a far sight from more affluent districts like the Gryphon's Roost. Further south, under the green-grey haze rising from quarries and ancryst processing facilities, the homes shrank and the buildings stretched into rows of unbroken brick with no yards or open space to speak of. Very much like Tane's neighborhood by the docks.

"This is the place," said Tane. He remembered the address from the records: 8 Thiel Street. The number was painted beside the door.

"You think Cranst hid portal here?" Kadka looked suspiciously at the brick building.

"No, but I think he might have chosen a place reasonably near. If he stole the badge, he would have wanted to be able to get to his hiding spot and back before Dedric noticed."

"So how do we find?"

"First, we wait for—"

Perfectly timed, a distant howling rose from the north, toward the Conservatory. The groan and crackle of ice was faint from this distance, but still noticeable—perhaps a little bit louder than what he'd heard through the portal, but he couldn't be certain.

"For that," Tane said. "What do you think? You have good ears. Was that closer or farther than what we heard in the workshop?"

"Closer, I think," said Kadka.

"Then we search southward, away from the park."

"What do we look for? Sound is not enough. Ears are not that good."

Tane pulled the watch case from his pocket and snapped it open to reveal the cloudy green ancryst held inside. "We use this. Ancryst makes a good magic detector, and the place should be warded against intrusion. The badge we found on Cranst was probably what he used to get in. So we circle these buildings front and back until the ancryst tells me there's a ward nearby, and then we look closer."

"Other magic won't move it? Magelights?"

"We'd have to be very close. It's going to react to a decent ward spell from much further away, and in a neighborhood like this, we're not likely to run into many of those. Too expensive to keep them up. Same reason I don't activate the ones on my office unless I know I'll need them. If the ancryst moves from the street or outside the yard, it's worth a closer look. There are going to be misleads, but I don't have a better way."

"Maybe Cranst is stupid, uses next house down."

"I don't think we're that lucky." Tane sighed. "This is probably going to take a while. Let's get started."

It was even slower work than Tane had expected. They moved down one street and up the next, checking each building as thoroughly as possible, but more than once they were driven off by residents who valued their privacy, or occasionally ones who just didn't like the look of Kadka's orcish features. Even when they weren't being chased, it was difficult to avoid attention from people sitting on stoops or going for an afternoon stroll. Kadka was usually able to sneak around the back fences to check the yards without being seen, but there was nowhere to hide in the street.

A few times the ancryst moved enough to be worth checking, but each time it was a false alarm: usually someone using some minor charm to banish a smell from their yard or clean their windows or the like, but once a gnomish child setting off colorful flash charms, all bright lights and loud popping sounds. That caught Tane by surprise, leaving him blinking away spots for several minutes.

Late afternoon was quickly becoming evening when Kadka called Tane around to the back of a seemingly empty home on Bolane Street, in a low brick building just like all the rest.

"Here, Carver. Stone is moving."

Tane ducked into the alley and found Kadka standing outside the fence of the second yard down. She handed him his watch case; he could feel it pushing against his palm.

"Boost me over," he said.

Kadka ducked down; Tane stepped into her cupped hands and vaulted the fence, landing roughly on his hands and knees. He lost his grip on his watch case, and an invisible force pushed the ancryst a foot or more toward the fence as it fell. *Definitely magic nearby.*

Kadka pulled herself over and landed easily on her feet as he retrieved the watch case. She pointed across the yard. "There, you think?"

Tane followed her finger to a pair of cellar doors set against the base of the building. He moved the ancryst from side to side, testing the direction of the force. "It's strongest in that direction." He stepped closer, and the force increased, until it threatened to push the case from his hand. When he snapped it closed, the pressure abated immediately, blocked by brass.

A chain held the doors shut, with a heavy iron lock at the center. Tane drew the key they'd found on Cranst from his pocket. Black iron, like the lock. He tried it—the key turned, and the lock opened.

"This is place, then," said Kadka.

Tane only nodded, his heart beating fast against his chest.

Kadka quickly pulled the chain free, and together they threw open the doors. A stone stair descended into the earth, with brick walls on either side. At the bottom, a hint of silver-blue magelight glimmered around the corner.

"Time to see what Cranst was hiding." Tane started forward.

"Wait," Kadka said, and caught him by the wrist. "Should be me. Might be other spell to see you, and then someone knows you are here. Won't see me."

Part of him wanted to argue—it felt like he'd come a very long way to get to this place, and he wanted to see it for himself. But Kadka was right. If there were any detection spells, she could walk through them freely. "Here," he said, and reluctantly handed her Cranst's crowned staff badge. "This should get you past any wards."

Kadka took the badge, and grinned. "Is good that I come now, yes?"

"Don't rub it in," Tane said, smiling slightly. "Just be careful, and tell me what you see as you see it."

Her grin widened. "If nothing kills me first."

With that, she started down the stairs.

At the bottom of the stairs, Kadka turned the corner into a room that made no sense to her at all.

The cellar was awash in silver-blue magelight cast by a glass globe hanging from the ceiling. Most of the floor was taken up by a strip of copper inlaid in the stone in a large circle. Glyphs she couldn't understand were scribed in gold across the copper band. On the far side stood a stone pedestal, about waist height, and from the top of the pedestal a bird-like copper claw jutted upward, holding a fist-sized gemstone of an opaque milky white. The gem was riddled with tiny cracks and chipped where pieces had fallen away. Lines of inlaid copper radiated from the base of the claw, one striking straight down to meet the copper circle and two more running to the other side of the pedestal, out of sight. Against the wall near the entryway where Kadka was standing, a little desk held a few books and a half-rolled paper.

"Don't know what this is, Carver, but looks like magic."

Carver's voice came from the top of the stairs. "Describe it to me."

"Is… big circle. Copper. Gold glyphs."

"Gold? They were trying to stabilize an unreliable spell. What else?"

"Pedestal at one side with white gem. Gem has little cracks, all over."

"The white is a sort of milky color?"

"Yes."

"How big?"

"Like fist."

"Spellfire." Carver sounded surprised. "A gem that size, and they used up all its power. How did Cranst pay for that?"

"Is desk here, with books. Let me check." The books had long titles that were nonsense to her, mostly Audish words she didn't know. She took one and opened it, looking for anything of interest.

"I took a peek through the window up here," Carver said from above as she flipped through pages. "There's nothing inside. Cranst must have rented this place just to use the cellar. Did you find anything else?"

The books meant very little to Kadka, and she didn't understand much of what she saw inside, but one word stood out. "Magic books, about portals."

"That makes sense, under the circumstances. Anything else?"

"Paper here too."

"What kind of paper?"

At one side of the desk was a large rectangular sheet, held in place in one corner with a brass paperweight. The other corners were free, and the sheet had been rolled closed to make room for the books. Kadka cleared the desk and flattened out the paper. It was covered in glyphs and complex instructions, but she recognized the diagram at the center easily enough. She'd seen it before, from across the Porthaven harbor.

"Plans for airship," she called to Carver.

"Really? I need to see that."

"Let me finish first. Might be more." She crossed the copper circle to the pedestal, tracing the copper lines inlaid in the marble. A glass-fronted cabinet was set into the far side. Inside was a scroll held between a pair of copper claws very much like the one holding the milky gem. The lines of copper from above each met a claw at its base.

Kadka knelt and opened the little glass door. "Is scroll in pedestal."

"Kadka, don't—"

She grabbed the scroll and lifted it from its housing. "Already took. Nothing happened."

"It might have been trapped!"

"Why trap when they think no one can get in?"

"I don't know, paranoia?" She heard him sigh, even from down the stairs and around the corner. "It doesn't matter now. I need a look at that scroll."

There didn't seem to be much else, which was disappointing. She'd been hoping for some magic she hadn't seen before. "Coming now."

Carver snatched the airship plans from her the moment she stepped out of the cellar.

"Now you say 'Thank you, Kadka,' yes?" she said, grinning.

"Thank you, Kadka," he repeated absently, without looking up. "These are for the envelope. The heating glyphs. That's what Thrung said Allaea was working on. This has to mean Cranst was planning to sabotage the launch." He beckoned for the other scroll. "Let me see that one."

Kadka handed it over. "Was in little copper hands. All joined up to circle."

He nodded. "That's not uncommon for a pre-cast spell. Engraving the glyphs is more permanent, but overly complex spells can be too long for that." He unrolled the scroll and started reading.

All the color left his face at once.

"Carver?"

"This is the flaw, Kadka. This is how they did it. Spellfire, I'm an idiot. What did I get us in to?"

As usual, she wasn't going to get any useful answers if she didn't ask. Carver was smart enough—when he wasn't being stupid, at least—but he took for granted a great deal of knowledge that she didn't have. Making him talk it through aloud seemed to help him find his way to the important parts. "Explain to me."

"This is a portal spell. It was all prepared in advance. The spell, the circle, that huge gem. Diamond, it says here, to provide the kind of power this would have taken. What we saw in the workshop wasn't a spell being cast in the moment. It was more like an artifact being activated." Carver touched the watch case in his pocket, the way she'd seen him do when he was agitated. "I should have seen it! I just never thought... portals are unstable, always shifting and changing. I've never heard of one being cast without direct oversight. I didn't know it could be done."

Kadka furrowed her brow. "So portal was made like artifact. This means something?"

"It means I've been working under a false assumption. Only the University heads can make a portal on campus, and they were all accounted for both times, so I accepted that they couldn't have done it. But *make* is the key. I told you the *lingua* is literal, and the glyph used in the portal ward refers to the actual effort of constructing the spell. As long as the right person *made* it, scribed the glyphs, invested their power into the gem... *anyone* could activate the portal, and the ward would allow it."

And now she understood. "This means a University head…"

"Was behind this all along," said Carver. "One of them put this portal together. And all four are going to have access to the airship tonight."

CHAPTER SIXTEEN

———

"THESE ARE POWERFUL people, Kadka," Tane said, weaving his way toward the lights of the ceremony through the crowd assembled along the harborfront. "And we're about to accuse one of them of a serious crime. They can make my life harder, but my reputation doesn't have far left to fall, and at least I have the protection of being born a citizen. You don't have that. If it goes badly, staying in the Protectorate might not be an option for you." Short of wrestling her to the ground and tying her up, there was no way to stop her from following—and he wouldn't win that contest. But at least he could warn her.

She wasn't ever going to *listen*, but he could warn her.

"You have bad memory, Carver. Same words, again and again." Kadka grinned. "Have to come, or I don't see what spell they try next to kill us."

"We both know I can't do much to stop you. I just thought you should know it could go worse for you than for me."

"Still. I go where you go."

"Have it your way." Tane sidestepped around a kobold woman who had stopped in the street to gawk at the lights.

The sun had set by the time they'd gotten off the
discs in Porthaven, and the launch ceremony was well
under way. Ahead, at the edge of the water by the
drydocked airship, the little park where launch ceremonies
were traditionally held had been transformed for the
occasion. Strings of hundreds of silver-blue magelights
held back the dark, and the area had been fenced off from
the surrounding harborfront and filled with silk-covered
tables and elegant flower arrangements.

Visible by its slight silver shimmer, a transparent barrier surrounded the entire affair to keep away any
unexpected weather, or unexpected guests. Within, the
city's elite mingled with foreign dignitaries, dancing and
laughing and probably making expensive deals and allianc-
es. And all along the waterfront outside, the less powerful
gathered to watch the launch, waiting excitedly for the
moment when the airship first took flight.

"Look, Carver." Kadka pointed upward, her eyes
wide—for a moment, orcish features or no, she fit perfectly with the rest of the awestruck crowd.

The airship itself didn't look much different from the
last time Tane had seen it, but the scaffolding was gone.
Now the great gleaming envelope loomed free over the
ceremony, unfettered save for the rigging linking it to the
hull. Several large magelights had been positioned beneath
so that it shone majestically against the night like a strange,
oblong moon, shedding reflected silver radiance across the
water. Why Lady Abena had chosen an evening launch,
Tane didn't know, but he supposed the airship *would* look
impressive shining over the harbor, and the lights of
Thaless equally so from above.

He kept moving. It was a lovely sight, but he didn't
have time for it.

Mageblades stood all around the perimeter of the
fence, holding back the crowd, and there was only one
point of entry to the ceremony: a white tent positioned
around the single gate, so that the unsightly business of

checking invitations and searching for weapons and arti-facts could be conducted without bothering those already inside. To one side of the entryway, dozens of guarded carriages sat waiting for their owners, most horse-drawn, but a few powered by ponderous, expensive ancryst en-gines. The wealthy didn't travel through Porthaven on foot, especially at night.

Tane strode directly to the tent, with Kadka just be-hind. Two Mageblades blocked his way, a handsome dark-haired elven man and a blonde human woman. Tane didn't let himself flinch. Any hesitation would only prove he didn't belong.

"Invitations?" the elf asked, eyeing the frayed edges of Tane's waistcoat and Kadka's tattered suspenders.

"I'm not a guest," said Tane. "But I am working at the request of Lady Abena. I have urgent information." By way of demonstration, he raised the portal scroll and airship plans rolled in his fist.

"No one gets in without an invitation. We're under strict orders."

"And you're doing a fine job. I know how important security is tonight, but this can't wait. Like I said, I'm working for the Lady Protector." Tane glanced theatrically to either side, leaned in, and lowered his voice. "Send to your commander. Say I need to speak with Inspector Indree Lovial. She's in charge of the covert detail from Stooketon Yard. The fact that I know that should tell you I'm not wasting your time. She'll vouch for me." He hated to bring Indree into it—she had more to lose than he did—but there wasn't much choice. He could worry about evading her once he was inside.

The elf lifted the graceful sweep of his eyebrow. "Sir, I don't think—"

"It's about the airship launch," said Tane. "If it goes wrong because I don't get in there, it's going to be on your heads. You don't want that. All you have to do is ask."

The two Mageblades shared a look, and then the

blonde woman's eyes focused on a distant point. After a
long silence, she nodded. "You'll be escorted to the inspector, but we'll have to search you first."

"Fine, just hurry. This is urgent."

The human woman pushed open the tent flap and
held it aside. "In here." She glanced at Kadka with some
distaste. "Your friend will have to wait."

"No, she's——" Tane stopped himself short. He might
have been able to persuade them, but he didn't *have* to.
And if Kadka wasn't going to listen to reason… "She's not
part of this. Just an escort to see me safely through the
crowd. You know how Porthaven can be at night."

Kadka's brow creased. "Carver?"

"Wait here, Kadka," he said, feigning an authoritarian
tone. "I won't need you inside."

She didn't argue. After everything they'd been
through together in the past few days, it might have been
easier if she had. Instead, she just looked at him. No sign
of the toothy grin he'd become accustomed to, but it
wasn't quite anger either. Just unblinking yellow eyes and a
straight, tight line to her mouth.

"I'm sorry," he whispered. "It's better this way."

And then he stepped into the tent, and left Kadka
behind.

The tent was lit inside by a single globe of magelight
suspended overhead. A pair of copper posts stood at the
mid-point of the space, one on the left and one on the
right, each topped with an unlit glass globe. A band of
glyphed copper ran across the ground between them,
perhaps six inches wide and long enough to span the tent
from side to side. Tane recognized the device at a glance: a
detection band, with a standard selection of security
divinations. When he stepped across the copper, the spells
would detect any Astrally charged artifacts he was carrying
and any brass that he might be using to hide them, as well
as a number of metals commonly used to forge weapons.
If he was carrying any of those things, the globes on either

side would fill with magelight. Two Mageblades were waiting on the far side to step in if necessary—a black-haired elven man and a red-scaled kobold.

"Please step through, sir," said the elf, and gestured at the detection band.

Tane did, and the magelights flared to life. No surprise, there. "I'm sorry," he said. "It must be this." He slipped the papers from Cranst's lair under his arm and took out his watch case, flipping it open to show the ancryst inside. It pulled against his grip, reacting to the presence of the detection spells behind him. At the same time, he slipped his left hand into his pocket and palmed the charmglobe within. "Brass, you know. Only a keepsake. No danger. Surely I don't have to leave it?"

"You can take it in with you, sir," said the kobold, hissing his 's' sounds. "But I have to ask you to step through the detections again without it first. We'll hold on to it for you."

The kobold approached with his hand out, and Tane took a sudden step forward, just a little bit too fast, so that they nearly collided. Tane reached out with his left hand to stop himself, and his fingers slid down the Mageblade's brass cuirass to surreptitiously deposit the charmglobe in the other man's pocket.

The kobold grabbed Tane's shoulder to steady him. "Careful."

"I'm sorry," Tane said, stepping back with a sheepish smile. "You'd think I'd gotten a head start on the festivities, but it's just clumsiness." He flipped the watch case closed and detached the chain from his waistcoat, then handed it over.

"Not a problem, sir. Please, step back through."

Tane stepped back across the detection band, and then forward again. The glass globes remained unlit.

It was easy enough to retrieve the charmglobe after the kobold gave him a final cursory pat down—pickpocketing was the most basic sleight of hand, and he'd used the same trick to get artifacts into exams a hundred times. He wasn't entirely certain why he'd done it *this* time, other than a strong feeling that he didn't want to go into this without any sort of defense. A simple flash charm wasn't much, but at least it was something.

The elven Mageblade escorted Tane across the ceremony grounds, keeping to the fence so as not to disturb the guests. Men and women in dress far finer than Tane's danced with one another further in, and others chatted at tables nearby. More than a few cast disparaging looks at his shabby clothes. He ignored the glances, and refastened his watch chain as he walked.

Halfway between the entry tent and the harborfront, Indree was leaning against the fence with one hand and holding a handbag in the other, watching the crowd. She wore a dress with a wine-red bodice and a long black skirt, and her black hair was elegantly done, swept up above her pointed ears in an elaborate knot of waves and curls. He'd never seen her like this before—at university, she'd stuck to the coats and trousers common among students.

She didn't turn as they approached, just waved off the Mageblade with a subtle gesture. "I'll take him from here. Keep moving, like you were just patrolling the perimeter." The dwarven man continued on with hardly a pause in his step.

Tane leaned his back against the fence beside her, trying not to draw attention. She was meant to blend in with the guests—best not to dispel the illusion. "You look very nice tonight," he said in a low voice. "Although I have to confess, I miss the badge and pistol."

She didn't look at him, but her cheeks flushed slightly. She pulled open the mouth of her handbag just enough that he could see the badge and ancryst pistol stowed inside. "I don't go anywhere without them. And speaking of badges"—a flash of annoyance in her eyes, there—"I suspect you have one that you shouldn't."

"Kadka has it, actually."

"But you did take it. Damn it, Tane, you'd better have found something good, or I swear by the Astra..." She glanced in his direction, and frowned. "Wait, where *is* Kadka? She's not with you?"

"We... decided it was better to split up. Cover more ground."

Indree rolled her eyes. "Which means you did something to chase her away. On the slim chance that you might actually listen to someone besides yourself: fix it. I like Kadka, and you two make a better team than common sense would suggest."

Tane rubbed the back of his neck. "It was the better plan. That's all."

"If you say so. Now, are you going to tell me why you're here?" She swept her gaze over the ceremony grounds as she spoke. "I have a job to do tonight. If you know something, get to it. Otherwise, let me work."

"It's nothing," Tane said, controlling his voice and his breath in case she tried a truth-spell. "I just had to use your name to get in. I'm not exactly on the list." He pulled the rolled papers from under his arm. "I got a sending from Dean Greymond. She wanted me to bring her some spell diagrams. Have you seen her?"

Now Indree turned fully toward him. "What diagrams?"

"Just some of the wards on the workshop. Maybe she's on to something for the investigation? I should probably go find her, in any case."

Her eyes narrowed. "Why are you lying to me, Tane?"

"What? I'm not..." But when he saw the look in her eyes, he gave it up. "How did you know? Truth-spell?"

"You'd just have beaten it. But it doesn't take a spell to see the holes in that story. Why would Greymond ask *you* to bring her these diagrams? And if she did, why didn't she arrange a way to get them to her without giving my name at the gate? You usually manage a better lie."

"In my defense, I don't know if there *was* a good lie for

this. I was hoping you wouldn't think too much about it."

"What's going on, Tane? The truth. Now. Or you go right back out the gate."

He'd had enough arguments with Indree to know she meant it, and if she threw him out, he wouldn't be getting back in. So he told her the truth. What he and Kadka had found in Cranst's bolthole and what it meant, with the spell diagram and the airship plans to support the story.

"Spellfire," Indree said softly. She'd turned away from the bulk of the crowd, hiding the spell scroll with her body as she looked it over. "One of the University heads? I don't want to believe it, but this spell... nothing else makes sense." She gave him a sidelong glance. "Why Greymond? You wanted to know where she was."

"Think about it. Cranst and his little cult were ready for us last night. There was only one person who knew where we were going." That had been on his mind since he and Kadka had found the portal diagram. He hated it, but it made sense.

"His cousin—"

Tane shook his head. "They were *waiting* for us. They knew exactly who was coming and when. Dedric couldn't have told them that much. Greymond could have. And it's not just that. She was awfully eager to blame Kivit Thrung for the murder, that first day. She only brought me in to try and prove he could have done it, and when I didn't, she immediately wanted me gone."

"That's... compelling, but it isn't proof," said Indree. She rolled up the scroll and tucked it into her bag along-side the airship plans. "If it's true, it means she's the one who sent Cranst. She's the reason Allaea's dead. I don't want to believe that. She was always so good to me. And she *adored* you, before... before everything."

"Do you think *I* want to believe it? I'm praying to the Astra that she has an explanation." However strained their relationship had become, it didn't change the fact that Liana Greymond had been an important part of his life once. He didn't want to believe she was capable of murder. "But it has to be one of the four of them, and right now she's at the top of the list."

Indree raised an eyebrow. "And if you'd managed to lose me and confront her alone, how exactly did you see it going? She could have easily had you thrown out. Or much worse, if you're right about this. She's a powerful mage, and you… aren't."

"There are a lot of people here. I thought if I could goad her into saying something she shouldn't, in front of witnesses…" Tane shrugged. "I would have had a plan by the time I found her."

"Here's one," said Indree. "*I'll* question her. I'm here at Lady Abena's request. She can't throw me out. Come on." She gestured to the tables nearest the water, where the most important guests were seated. "I don't think she's much of a dancer. She probably hasn't left the faculty table."

"Wait." Tane grabbed her arm. "Accusing a dean of murder could get you demoted or worse. Please, just… let me do this. I don't have as much at stake."

Indree jerked her arm away and rounded on him, anger flashing in her amber eyes. "Hard as it may be for you to believe, not everything is a puzzle that only the brilliant Tane Carver can solve! I didn't join the constabulary just to have the shiniest badge, and you *know* that! Stop pretending—" She stopped herself, sucked in a breath through gritted teeth. "If Greymond means to sabotage the airship, it's my duty to stop her. You can be part of it or not, but I don't have time to do this with you." And then she was pushing her way through the crowd, and he had no choice but to follow.

Greymond was sitting with Dean Brassforge and Dean Orthea around a table near the water, leaning forward in animated discussion. As Tane and Indree approached, he became aware of a number of other guests moving in from all sides. None of them stood out particularly—they were dressed in much the same evening finery as everyone else—but several slipped hands into handbags or topcoats as they drew near. Reaching for badges, or perhaps pistols. Indree must have sent to the rest of her detail for support.

Indree hadn't yet announced herself, and she was still ten steps back when Greymond stood bolt upright and whirled around, eyes wide.

It wasn't easy to take a diviner by surprise.

But Greymond didn't run. Her hands shook as she raised them. "You think I... No! I would never!"

"What is this, Liana?" Dean Orthea asked, her perfect brow creasing slightly. She pushed back her chair and made to stand to her full eight foot height.

Indree drew her badge from her purse and flashed it quickly before hiding it once more. The rest of her detail closed in to surround the table. "I'm going to have to ask all three of you to stay where you are for a moment," she said. Orthea frowned, but took her seat once more. "I'm sorry for the disturbance. Dean Greymond, I have to ask—"

"I wasn't part of this, Inspector Lovial, I promise you!" Greymond's voice was high and the words came too fast. "Ask whatever you need to ask to believe me, cast any spells you must. I would never put any of my students in danger!"

Tane stepped forward. "But you wanted me—"

"I only asked for your help with Mister Thrung because there were no other suspects, and I had to know if he could have bypassed the wards. I admit I... I didn't want you involved after that, but only because of our history. Tane, you must know I wouldn't do this!" And she *did* seem genuinely panicked—if it was an act, he couldn't see through it.

Indree was watching her closely too, with that faraway diviner's look in her eye. "And what about—"

"I swear by the Astra, I didn't warn Cranst you were coming!"

"No one else knew, Liana," said Tane. "How—"

"I don't know! I…" And then all the color fled her cheeks at once. "I only told one person."

"Who?" Indree demanded, but by the look on her face, she'd already guessed the answer, just as Tane had.

Fear dawning in her eyes, Greymond said the only name she could have said:

"Chancellor Nieris."

CHAPTER SEVENTEEN

FOR A MOMENT, Tane didn't believe her. He *wanted* to, but it felt too easy. Greymond's only way out was to blame someone else, and Brassforge and Orthea were at the table, so it had to be Nieris. If there was a more transparent excuse, he couldn't think of it.

Except... there was something there, a hint of memory at the back of his mind.

Indree raised an eyebrow, outwardly skeptical. "You told—"

"Of course I did!" Greymond exclaimed, drawing glances from the surrounding guests. "He's the chancellor of the University! Why wouldn't I update him on the investigation?"

The sculpture. That was it. The Mage Emperor's crowned staff, wrought in bronze, sitting in plain sight in the chancellor's office. The same symbol as the one on Cranst's badge.

If it was true, it would be almost unbelievably arrogant for Nieris to put his true allegiance on display like that, but it also made a strange kind of sense. He was three hundred years old, chancellor of the most prestigious university of magic in the world for more than a century, among the most experienced mages alive. He dressed in clothes that princes of Rhien might have found a bit much. If any man had ever had reason to believe himself untouchable, it was Talain Nieris. Of *course* he wouldn't hide who he was—he would show the world, and laugh when no one noticed.

"There is no mage alive with as much experience in portal magic," Tane said softly.

Indree glanced sidelong at him. "What?"

"That's what Nieris said about himself, that first day in his office. Spellfire, he might as well have been *bragging* about it."

"So you believe her?"

"I think I do," said Tane. "Nieris could have warned Cranst, if Greymond was reporting our movements to him. He's the one who said the howling Kadka and I heard was nothing, which is why we ignored it for so long—he was the expert, after all. By his own admission, he knows portal magic better than anyone. Who better to come up with this particular plan? And he was so *keen* to blame Cranst and bury any problems with the wards, as long as the launch wasn't delayed. I thought it was just typical University arrogance and bureaucracy, but if he means to sabotage the airship…"

Indree prodded her tongue with her cheek, thinking it over. "But why bother sending Cranst through a portal at all? If the chancellor of the University wanted airship plans, he could have just walked in and looked at them."

"But he couldn't have *done* anything with them. The workshops were under guard. If he was seen coming and going, and then something went wrong with the airship, he'd be on the list of suspects. This way it could have been done without anyone noticing, and if someone did, he had an alibi. He made sure he and all the deans were accounted for, so we had to assume the portal wards had been beaten some other way." The last piece fell into place then, the one thing he hadn't been able to explain before.

"*That's* what Cranst was receiving. Not instructions—new diagrams. He sent them out to Nieris the first time, when he killed Allaea. The second time, he wasn't taking anything. He was replacing the original plans with ones Nieris sent him."

"Then what are these?" asked Indree, tapping a finger against the airship plans poking from her handbag.

"The originals," said Tane. "They must be. Cranst couldn't leave them behind, or someone would have noticed there were duplicates. He must have taken them the day Kadka and I found him in the workshop."

"This is absurd," interrupted Dean Brassforge. "You're saying my airship plans were replaced? By the *chancellor?* Which plans? Why?"

"The heating glyphs for the envelope," said Tane. "They wanted diagrams for vital airship spells, and Allaea would have had these ones out already. After she alerted the guard, there wasn't time to search for more." And then the full implication hit him. "Spellfire, Nieris was never planning to sabotage the airship *at* the ceremony. He's already done it. If Cranst made the exchange, then the final heating glyphs came from *their* diagram, not Allaea's!"

"Impossible!" said Brassforge, his cheeks flushing beneath his auburn beard. "We would have noticed—"

"Would you?" Tane rounded on Brassforge, his voice rising. He'd seen this happen before—it was the ancryst rail all over again. "The spell diagrams were already finalized. That's why Cranst chose that evening—no one should have been working on them by then. Tell me, Dean Brassforge, after you'd given your approval, would you have been the one looking at those plans? Do you and your mages tend to build your ancryst machines with your own hands?"

Brassforge—never particularly verbose—could only stammer under Tane's sudden anger. "I... We don't—"

"No. You *don't.* Workers and engineers and mechanics do that part, and none of them have any magecraft. By now they'll have scribed the glyphs exactly as the diagram says, because how would they know not to? You say you would have noticed, but the truth is that if it wasn't for Allaea working too late that night, you'd never have known anything was wrong!"

"I told her," Indree whispered. "I told her she was giving too much time to those stupid glyphs." And then she set her jaw, slung her handbag over her shoulder, and drew her pistol from within. "We need to find Nieris. He does *not* get away with this." Looking to the deans, she demanded, "Where is he?"

Dean Orthea looked entirely lost, her lovely lips hanging agape. "He... He was here earlier, but we haven't seen him for... a quarter hour, perhaps. He was with Lady Abena."

"Let me," Greymond said. Her eyes clouded for a moment, and then she frowned. "I... can't locate either of them. They're nearby, but their Astral signatures are clouded."

"Spellfire!" Indree swore. "He must have seen us already. And if the Lady Protector is masked too... damn it, he has her!" She swept her eyes over the disguised constables surrounding the table. "I want all eyes looking for the chancellor and Lady Abena. And tell any Mageblades you find to get word to their commander: we need them to ground that airship."

"Wait," Tane said, and Indree looked at him, raising a hand to belay her order. "That's it, Indree. The *airship*. If Nieris thinks we're coming for him, that's where he'll be. He knows he can't wait for the launch anymore—he's going to have to do it himself!"

"Come on!" Indree was already moving, hitching up her dress and sprinting toward the drydock at the edge of the ceremony grounds, where the airship sat waiting. Tane and the rest of her detail followed behind.

A pair of human Mageblades stood guard over the ramp leading to the steel entry hatch in the airship's side. It stood open, ready for boarding during the launch ceremony. The wood-and-steel hull towered overhead, braced in the drydock, and at this distance the light reflecting from the envelope cast everything in shimmering silver.

The Mageblades moved to block the ramp as they approached, and both put hands to their pistols when they saw Indree's already drawn.

"Stop!" called the man on the left, bald and broad-shouldered. "Drop your weapon!"

Indree held up her badge. "Constable Inspector Indree Lovial. Have you seen the Lady Protector?"

The second Mageblade, a sturdy brown-haired woman, nodded her head. "She just came aboard, with Chancellor Nieris. What is this about?"

"We have reason to believe the chancellor may mean her harm," said Indree. "I'm going to need you to let us by. Send to your commander. Tell him to get everyone here, right now. We have to clear the airship and keep it grounded."

"Lady Abena didn't show any sign of distress," the bald man said. "We were told the chancellor had something to show her before the launch. She left orders not to let anyone—"

"I'm not just *anyone*," said Indree. "The Lady Protector personally asked me to lead this detail. We don't have time for this!"

"I'm sorry, ma'am, but we need authorization from Commander Tavis to let you on board," the bald man said flatly.

"So get it! Isn't that what I *just* asked you to do?" Exasperation colored Indree's voice. "If he doesn't believe me, tell him to try and contact Lady Abena. He'll find someone is masking her."

The bald man nodded at his partner; she concentrated a moment, and then her eyes glazed with the sending.

Tane shifted his feet impatiently as the woman questioned Indree and relayed the answers to her commander.

This was taking too long, and Nieris wasn't going to wait for their convenience. He'd been trying very hard not to think of Kadka—of the way she'd looked at him when he left her behind—but in that moment he couldn't help it. *She wouldn't have any patience for this*. And he could imagine very easily what she'd have done in his place. He glanced at the female Mageblade's clouded eyes, and then down to her waist, where a pair of ancryst pistols were slung over either hip.

There was one sure way to make the Mageblades seize the airship.

They just needed an obvious threat.

The woman was still distracted by her sending when Tane darted forward. He shouldered her to one side and lifted a pistol from her hip in a single motion. The bald Mageblade jabbed out a hand to grab him. Tane felt fingers brush his back, but they found no purchase, and then it was too late. He was already by, sprinting up the ramp.

"Stop!" the Mageblade bellowed, and then a sound of metal on leather—almost certainly an ancryst pistol being drawn. "One more step and I'll shoot!"

Tane ducked his head, and kept running.

"Wait!" Indree's voice. A quick flurry of noise, and then a startled grunt. A pistol-ball threw splinters from the wooden hull ahead, significantly off-target.

Footsteps behind, then, moving quickly. They were following. Good. Close at his back, someone was chanting words in the *lingua*, but spells took time, and it wasn't a terribly long ramp. He was nearly at the door.

Astra, please just keep them from shooting me for a little bit longer.

This had to be the stupidest thing he'd ever done. Even if he *didn't* get himself killed, there would be consequences later. But if it got Indree and the Mageblades on board before Nieris launched the ship, it would be worth it. Sometimes talking worked, or knowledge, or clever tricks, but sometimes there was only Kadka's way: charge at the problem with your teeth bared and punch it in the throat.

Tane lunged through the door into the body of the airship. A short magelit hall led further in, with a brass railing running down both sides. It branched in three directions just ahead; he started toward the junction. He had to lead them to the bridge—that was where Nieris would be, if he meant to launch the ship.

A loud thud and clang from behind stopped him in his tracks. He knew what it was even before he turned. *No. Not now.*

The hatch was closed, slammed shut by some invisible force. He was alone.

The floor lurched beneath his feet.

The airship began to rise.

———

Kadka stalked along the fence just outside the perimeter established by the Mageblades.

A crowd of onlookers milled about in her path, pointing and gawking up at the airship—the first time she'd seen the people of Thaless react properly to an obvious wonder of magic. When they saw her coming, most took one look at her face and gave her ample room to pass. They saw an orc, and they moved in the other direction. Not very nice, but useful just then. If they didn't get out of the way, she pushed them aside herself, which did nothing to stop the nervous looks aimed at her.

But she was used to that. It wasn't resentment driving her forward, it was urgency. She needed to find a way into the ceremony, and there wasn't any time to waste. Carver was *going* to get himself in trouble, and if she wasn't there…

Carver. That *vekad* fool of an idiot. Too clever to realize how stupid he was. She'd never been quick to anger, but when she found him again, he'd be lucky if she didn't break his nose.

He didn't get to decide she wasn't a part of this anymore. She'd witnessed magic in these last few days she never would have seen standing watch over doors all day. People had tried to kill her, and that needed answering. She wasn't ready for it to be over. She wasn't *done*.

She'd circled almost all the way around the fence now, drawing near the drydock where the airship waited. She couldn't see any break in the security. For a moment, she considered diving into the harbor to approach from the water, where the Mageblades were fewer. But even if she wasn't seen, she would still have to contend with the dome of magical energy over the ceremony grounds.

She wasn't done, but she couldn't see any way forward, either.

As consolation, she allowed herself a brief glance up at the airship's shining envelope. At least she'd gotten to see it like this, illuminated by magelight, reflecting silver radiance all across the harborfront. It was beautiful against the starlit sky.

And it was moving.

Kadka blinked, squinted her eyes. Had she imagined it? No, it was moving, lifting out of the drydock. The activity among the crowd intensified—frantic gestures, cries and shouts of "*It's starting!*" and "*Look, son, this is it!*"

They thought this was the launch, happening as scheduled. But something was wrong.

The airship was still tethered.

The first line broke free on the corner of the drydock nearest Kadka, and then another followed, and another. The airship rose slowly, moving away from the harbor toward the city. The Mageblades were mobilizing now, pushing people out of the ship's path, but there was little they could do—they were as helpless to stop it as everyone else.

One of the broken tether-lines drifted by over Kadka's head, and she followed without thinking. She only knew two things: first, that the airship wasn't supposed to be moving; second, that if it was, Carver was probably on board, and in some kind of danger.

And as much as she wanted to kick him in the head just then, he was going to need her.

The tether-line was already a full body-length above her, but she sprinted after it anyway, picking up speed as she moved. A towering ogren in a gryphon-etched Mageblade cuirass was trying to clear the crowd; he saw her coming, and stepped into her path. Kadka didn't slow down.

"Stop, ma'am," the ogren ordered in a deep, harmonious voice. He bent to catch her, a nine-foot statue carved of flawless marble dropping to one knee. "You need to clear—"

Kadka bared her teeth in a wide grin and jumped straight at him. The ogren's eyes widened in surprise. She kicked off his grasping arm—startlingly firm and strong under her feet—and bounded to the lowered shoulder of his brass cuirass like she was climbing a staircase. He straightened, lifting her higher still as he reached up to grab her.

He was too late.

Arms outstretched, Kadka leapt for the trailing tether-line.

CHAPTER EIGHTEEN

———

TANE'S STOMACH LEAPT into his throat as the floor shook and swayed underfoot. His vision spun. He hated travelling by ancryst machine at the best of times; this might well have been the worst. He thrust the stolen ancryst pistol into his pocket and grasped the brass rail that ran along the hall to keep himself upright.

Pressure built in his ears, and then a voice from nowhere spoke in his head. *"Mister Carver. I hoped you would come."*

The pressure didn't abate; the link was still open. *"Nieris."* Tane clenched his eyes shut and touched the watch case in his waist pocket with two fingers, but the voice he sent was as calm as he could manage. *"What do you want?"*

"For you to join me and the Lady Protector on the bridge. She would very much appreciate if you came quickly and agreeably."

"Because you'll hurt her if I don't, you mean?" The pressure of the sending was making his nausea worse; sweat beaded on his forehead. But still, he didn't let Nieris hear it. *"Why mince words at this point?"*

"I am a civilized man, Mister Carver. I dislike making vulgar threats. Please, don't keep us waiting."

Tane's ears popped, and the presence in his head was gone. Gasping with relief, he slumped to the floor and put his back to the wall. His head dropped between his knees, and he held it there until his breathing slowed.

Collect yourself, Carver. Lady Abena's life is at stake. He pushed himself upright and grabbed hold of the rail, gripping it with white-knuckled desperation. *At least I won't fall on my ass if—* Something shook the airship; the hall moved suddenly underfoot. He clutched tight to the rail and rode it out. *I swear by the Astra, if I survive this, I'm never setting foot on an airship again.*

Shuffling along the rail, he started down the hall that he guessed would bring him toward the bridge. A stairway at the far end led to an upper level.

He hadn't gone far when the pressure in his ears returned. *Astra, not again.*

"Tane!" Indree's voice. That wasn't so bad. *"I couldn't reach you! I thought... Are you alright?"*

"I'm on the first flight of an untested, presumably sabotaged airship," he answered, continuing on past the heavy steel hatches that lined the hall on both sides. *"I wouldn't say I'm alright. But I'm not hurt."*

"Good." A pause, and then, *"You Astra-riven idiot. What were you thinking?"*

"That we were taking too long to get aboard. Looks like I was right."

"Of course. Getting yourself locked in a stolen airship with the most powerful mage in Thaless was obviously *the right decision."* If she'd been there with him, she'd have been glaring in that way only she could. He could almost see it—like she meant to flay the skin from his bones with her eyes alone. *"Have you heard from Nieris? Was it him blocking my sending before?"*

"He has Lady Abena. I'm supposed to come to him on the bridge." He reached the stairs and started up, taking great care with each step. His hands never left the rail.

"You have to stall him. We're still trying to find a way to board."

He didn't have high hopes. Mages could levitate, but not at speed, and a portal into a moving target was dangerous and impractical. *"I'll try,"* he said. *"What about the heating glyphs? Whatever Nieris did, it might be reversible. If you can get the altered plans from the shipyard—"*

"Already done. Dean Brassforge is looking over the glyphs now."

"Tell me as soon as he finds something." Tane crested the stairway to find another four-way junction in the hall. *"I think… I think I see the bridge."* Ahead, straight through the junction, the hall ended in a large steel hatch with a round window. In the room beyond, a huge half-circle of glass panes looked out onto the deck. A panel of levers and glyphed instruments sat below, with a large ship's wheel at its center.

He couldn't see anyone, but Nieris had to be inside somewhere. Tane reached into his pocket and wrapped his fingers around the ancryst pistol's grip.

"Just keep him talking while we figure out how to get to you, Tane," Indree sent, and in that moment he was all too aware of just how far away and below she was. *"Don't make him angry. As much frustration as it might save me, I don't want you getting yourself killed."*

"I'll try not to—" He neared the hatch, and the sending-pressure abated before he could finish. Indree wouldn't have cut him off like that—this was something else. He'd come within range of Nieris' masking spell.

The handle on the hatch turned itself, and the door opened. Nieris' voice came from over the threshold. "Mister Carver. I'm so glad you've decided to join us. Please, come in."

Tane stepped through the hatch. The tingle of a ward raised the hair on his arms.

Talain Nieris stood in front of the instrument panel a few feet to the right of the wheel. Through the half-circle of windows behind him, the lights of Thaless shone against the dark. He held his head high, his shoulders square, his hands clasped at his back—the picture of elven refinement and poise. A perfectly pressed indigo topcoat with black lapels draped perfectly over his shoulders, with trousers to match, and a deep violet cravat at the neck, impeccably tied and ruffled. His short black hair was neatly parted, not a strand out of place; the hint of grey above his pointed ears only made him look more distinguished. He might have been a gentleman receiving an honored guest, rather than the dangerous criminal he was.

The Lady Protector wasn't with him.

"Nieris. Where—"

Without moving or even unclasping his hands, Nieris uttered a single word in the *lingua*. Before Tane could react, a band of silver-blue force wrapped around his midsection, binding his arms to his sides and lifting him from his feet. The spell pushed him hard against the back wall, and pinned him there, a foot above the floor. He struggled, but the Astral energy held him fast. This was too complex a spell for so few words—it must have been spoken in advance and held for completion. One of the most difficult tricks of magecraft, especially while concentrating on other spells. Nieris looked like a bit of a dandy, but he had three hundred years of magical experience, and that made him exceptionally dangerous.

And now Tane saw Lady Abena pinned to the same wall just to his right, her arms likewise constrained with silver-blue magic. Her ceremony attire was considerably less neat than Nieris', a rumpled white coat-dress accented with Audish blue, rucked up at the sleeves where the band of force held her arms.

She offered him a wan smile. "Mister Carver. I don't suppose you brought any friends?" Capture, it seemed, hadn't diminished her composure.

"It's just me, I'm afraid," said Tane. His fingers were still wrapped tight around the pistol in his pocket, but it wasn't going to do him much good with his arms bound below the elbow.

Nieris raised an eyebrow. "Not even that... *thing* that has been following you all over the city?" His lip twisted with distaste. "There is no purpose in lying, Mister Carver. I may not be able to detect her, but she cannot pass through the ward I've cast on this room. She won't be coming to help you."

"I don't know where Kadka is. We... parted ways." Tane tried, without much success, to focus on Nieris rather than the nighttime glow of the city glimmering through the half-circle of the bridge windows. The lights were too small, too far below.

"An act of surprising good taste, if true," said Nieris. "I don't know how you could stand to be near such an unnatural creature. It is one thing to be magicless, another to be *absent* from the Astra. I've never seen the like, and I have dealt with full-blooded orcs more than once. But I suppose as a non-magical yourself, you are blind to such things. I admit, it was a great relief when you supplied me with a reason to remove her from the Guard."

"So you owe me a favor," said Tane. "Let us go and set down the airship, and we'll call it even." The airship shuddered, and a long groan sounded from somewhere above. He swallowed, and his fingers twitched instinctively toward his waist pocket, but he couldn't reach.

Nieris chuckled. "Even now you insist upon your little jests. I must say, Mister Carver, you have impressed me. When I allowed you to work on the investigation, I believed that a man without magic could only get in the way of the constabulary. But you persevered, and here we are. Perhaps I should even thank you. You see, it occurred to me after you dealt with poor Randolf that I would need a new scapegoat. And you offered yourself up so nicely."

"It's too late to put the blame on me, Nieris. I've already told the constabulary everything."

"I'm sure you've told them quite a tale," said Nieris. "A pity that in a short while you will not be available to argue your case." He smiled, a menacing glint in his sapphire-blue eyes. "You see, Mister Carver, this airship is about to fall out of the sky. With you on board."

CHAPTER NINETEEN

KADKA CLUNG TO the side of the rapidly ascending airship, clutching the tether-line tight in her fist as the ground dropped away beneath her. She had to be hundreds of feet up already, and still rising. The air was growing colder, and a rising wind whipped through the hair on her head and the backs of her hands, threatening to tug her away into open sky if she loosened her grip for even a moment.

It was incredible.

She could see all of Thaless spread across the coast below, a city mapped in landmarks of light and dark. Yellow-orange oil lamps at the outer edges transitioned to silver-blue magelight in the wealthier central districts. There in the middle of it all was the great dome of the Brass Citadel, the seat of the Protectorate's government, divided into pie-slice segments by a framework of silver lights embedded from tip to base. Just south of that was the great expanse of Rosepetal Park, a broad swath of untouched natural darkness. Further north, the illuminated face of the clock tower above Thalen's Hall marked the University campus. Craning her neck back, she could still see a dense collection of magelights at the edge of the harbor behind her—the ceremony grounds, getting further and further away as the airship drifted inland over the city.

She climbed hand over hand up the rope, stopping to anchor herself on the sill of a porthole whenever the wind gusted too strong or the ship swayed too heavily. Now and again, a strange, straining groan came from the shimmering silver envelope overhead. It didn't sound very good, but then, she didn't know what sound an airship was *supposed* to make. It might have been the result of some kind of sabotage; it might have been nothing at all.

Either way, it was enough to make her climb faster.

The tether-line was tied off to a heavy iron ring a few feet below the deck—just far enough that she couldn't reach the edge to pull herself up. There were no handholds across that final gap, just the sealed wood of the hull.

But she wasn't about to stop here. There was still one way up.

Kadka took a final look down at the beautiful lightscape below, gripped the ring with both hands, tensed her arms, and hurled herself upward.

For a moment, she was suspended in open air, a thousand feet above the ground, at the mercy of wind and gravity. Flying, almost. She laughed aloud, terrified and exhilarated at once. With straining fingers she reached for the edge of the deck. The fingertips of her right hand grazed the edge, caught...

And slipped away.

"*Deshka!*" she swore, and grasped wildly with her left hand. Two fingers hooked over the side, no further than the second joint. Not enough to support her weight, but in that brief moment of stability, she gathered her feet under her and kicked blindly for the iron ring below. Her right foot found purchase. She pushed off, just high enough to get her elbow over the edge above. With her right hand, she reached up again and gripped a brass support of the deck rail. A moment later she was pulling herself over to safety.

She collapsed on the deck, her heart pounding, and rolled onto her back. For a moment she just looked up at the great silver oval shining above and tried to catch her breath.

And then that groan came again, louder and longer. Something wasn't right.

Kadka pushed herself up and looked along the deck. Just ahead, near the front of the ship, a half-circle of windows framed a room that had to be important. There were lights inside, casting moving shadows over the deck.

Someone was there.

She crept closer, staying low, until she was crouched beneath the nearest window. Showing as little of herself as she could manage, she peeked in the bottom corner.

She'd been right about Carver—he'd gotten himself in trouble. He was pinned against the wall by some kind of spell, a band of silver-blue force around his torso and arms. Lady Abena was beside him, likewise trapped. And though the mage holding them in place had his back to her, Kadka knew him. Pointed elven ears, greying temples, expensive clothing with frills at the sleeve and neck—he was hard to mistake.

Chancellor Nieris.

Kadka was less surprised than she should have been. For all his forced politeness, she'd seen the ugliness beneath when the chancellor had looked at her, the glint of pleasure in his eyes when he'd stripped her of her badge. He wasn't the first to look at her that way, and probably not the last, but she always noticed. She hadn't suspected him of worse only because he'd seemed too much the fancy bookish sort to get his hands dirty.

Apparently she'd misjudged him, there. But nowhere else.

And now he had Carver, and the Protector of the Realm. She had to help them, but how? There was a door just to her right, but it was thick steel, and turning the wheel to open it would draw too much attention. Breaking a window would be no better. If Nieris heard her coming, she'd have to cross the room faster than he could cast a spell, and he had three hundred years of experience doing just that. And even if she *could* get in quietly, he might well already have wards in place to stop her. She'd learned some about magic over the last few days, but not enough to find the flaws the way Carver could.

So Carver would have to do it for her. If she was going to save him, he'd have to help her do it.

She just had to get his attention first.

———

"What did you do, Nieris?" Tane demanded. His only chance now was to keep Nieris talking until help came—*if* help was coming. "It's the heating glyphs, isn't it?"

"Astute, Mister Carver," Nieris said with a condescending smirk. "A shame such a mind was wasted on a non-magical. Yes, I altered Miss Hesliar's work on the glyphs. A minor change to the limits on their power consumption. Or rather, a complete removal. But the engravers had no means to catch such a mistake, as you well know. And now the envelope is overheating above us, expanding beyond its capacity. The higher we go, the further it stretches. You've already heard it groaning under the strain, I expect. Very soon…" Nieris clasped his hands together and then parted them suddenly, pantomiming an explosion.

"This is madness, Talain!" said Lady Abena, pulling against her magical bonds. "If we crash over the city… there are people down there asleep in their homes! They'll be killed!"

"Yes," Nieris said. "And then your airship will be nothing but a failed experiment. How could the project go on, after such tragedy?"

Lady Abena ceased her struggles, and looked, aghast, to the chancellor. "You'll die just as surely as anyone!"

"You think so little of me, Your Ladyship?" Nieris affected a tone of mild indignation. "I assure you, I will survive. You forget: I am the most accomplished portal mage alive."

"You're going to portal out of a moving ship?" Tane's incredulity was only partly feigned to keep Nieris talking. "That *is* insane. There's no way to anchor it!" A portal linked two fixed points in space—it wouldn't be able to move with the ship.

"Ah, the limited vision of the magicless." The chancellor preened a bit, grasping his lapel with one hand. "I only need to anchor this end at the moment of entry, Mister Carver. The casting *can* be done in motion, and the position fixed only at the last instant. Then I simply need to step through before the ship moves away. Perilous for the untrained, but for a master of the craft? Easily done."

It *was* theoretically possible, but it would make an already unstable spell even more unreliable. "If you get it wrong and miss your jump, the portal will tear the hull apart as the ship moves by," Tane said. "We all die, and who knows what comes out of the Astra. Directly over Thaless."

"True," Nieris said without apparent concern. "But I have no intention of making such an amateur mistake." The arrogance of it was astounding, and Tane was no stranger to arrogance.

"*Why*, Talain?" Lady Abena demanded. "Why are you doing this? You've served the Protectorate faithfully for centuries!"

"Precisely," said Nieris. "Centuries, watching the nation I have devoted my life to make the same mistake, again and again. I am a scion of House Nieris and the greatest mage of our time, and yet I am forced to suborn myself to an endless parade of magicless fools calling themselves Protectors of the Realm. And all because I was born with a power that makes me their *better!*" For a moment, his mannered veneer peeled aside; he spat the last word with a grimace of disgust. "And now you would ally with the people of the Continent. With these barbarians who fear everything that magic can do, who have sought to destroy us for centuries. Your peace will not last. They will take these airships you mean to give them, and turn them against us. I will *not* allow that to happen. The time has come to make the Mage Emperor's dream a reality. Your demise with your airship will be a symbol: a new age is dawning, and the magical will rule!" He raised his fist with all the zeal of a preacher in the Halls of the Astra, and looked to his captives as if expecting applause.

"You're mad," said Lady Abena. "The moment they see a new Mage Emperor rising to power, every nation on the Continent will move against us. We can't fight them all, Talain. The Protectorate will be wiped from the map."

"Spoken like a non-magical. You haven't the faintest idea what a mage is *truly* capable of." Nieris looked at her for a long moment; his eyes clouded over slightly. "Let me show you."

And then Lady Abena screamed.

She writhed wildly against her bonds, her eyes rolling back in her head, her neck cording with the strength of her screams. Nieris had to be sending her pain—or maybe that wasn't strong enough. This was more like agony, and not just a short burst of it like Tane had gotten from Cranst. No one could suffer like that for very long.

"Stop it!" Tane shouted. "You'll kill her!"

Lady Abena gave a final heave against her bonds, and slumped limply forward. Nieris' eyes focused once more, and he released her, letting her fall to the ground.

Tane stared at her, wide-eyed. "Is she…"

"She lives," said the chancellor, looking contemptuously at the Lady Protector. "For now." His eyes moved to Tane, considering. Overhead, the envelope groaned once more, long and loud.

Spellfire! If he's willing to do that to the most powerful woman in the Protectorate, he isn't going to balk at me. Tane blurted the first thing that came to mind as a distraction, hoping

Nieris' pride would demand he answer. "You must know you can't get away with this! You've already made too many mistakes. You trusted Cranst, and he let himself be seen. This won't look like an accident, now that everyone is looking for a crime."

Nieris took a long breath, visibly collecting his calm, and clasped his hands behind his back once more. "Yes, poor Randolf did make rather a mess of things, didn't he? But don't confuse his mistakes for mine. You know, he didn't even tell me that you had taken the scrollcaster at first. I had to confront him after Dean Greymond told me about your 'black market contacts'. He wanted to fix his failure himself, I suppose. He was so eager to make it up to me—how could I deny him the chance?"

It wasn't hard to find the meaning in that. "You told him to kill himself. He did it for you."

"I thought perhaps the investigation would end with him. And it might have, if not for you and that orcish aberration."

"But the bluecaps know about you now. Even if you portal away, they know you're behind this!"

"No," said Nieris. "They only know that you claim I am. They cannot catch us in time to stop me now, and afterward, all the witnesses will be dead—who's to say I was ever aboard? I will claim that I slipped away in the confusion of a madman taking the ship. I have powerful friends who will vouch for me. And the infamous Tane Carver *was* seen wandering about the University shortly after the murder, and boarding this airship just before it took flight. Seeking vengeance for his expulsion, I shouldn't wonder. Given your reputation, who will believe your story against mine? Not many, I suspect, considering you will not be alive to argue the point."

"Indree will never accept that."

"Inspector Lovial will do what her superiors tell her, or surrender her badge. Enough of this, Mister Carver. I know you are trying to delay me. It is amusing that you think I can be so easily fooled. I didn't come this far only to leave you with enough time to ground the airship after I am gone. I have simply been waiting for the point of no return." Another great moan came from the envelope. Textile stretching, metal bending and buckling. "I believe we are past that now." Nieris turned away to face the right wall, and began to chant under his breath. Tane recognized the words of the *lingua*—he was casting his portal.

"Wait! I—"

Nieris didn't even look at him, just flicked his fingers and uttered a few short words. A muzzle of silver-blue force surrounded Tane's jaw, clamping it shut.

Astra, what am I supposed to do now? The flash charm loaded in his charmglobe was a momentary distraction at best, and the stolen pistol in his pocket was useless. Even if he could fumble it out and shoot from the wrist with true enough aim to hit anything, casting a portal took more than enough Astral energy to turn an ancryst ball aside. And no aid was coming. Nieris had been right about that. There was no way for the bluecaps or Mageblades to get aboard. Casting a portal *from* the ship was one thing— opening one *into* a moving target would be impossible.

Tane watched helplessly as the chancellor uttered his portal spell, bringing a silver-blue shimmer of magic into the world near the right wall. It shifted and grew from the size of his fist to the size of his head and then larger still. It wasn't a true portal yet—nothing was visible on the other side—but it wouldn't be long. *I can't stop him. I'm going to die here.*

And then, behind Nieris' back on the left side of the bridge, he saw something. Movement. He couldn't turn his head far under the constraint of the muzzle, but he shifted his eyes.

Kadka stared back at him through the window, waving her arms over her head to get his attention.

CHAPTER TWENTY

IF TANE HADN'T been muzzled, he might have cheered. He'd never been so happy to see anyone in his life.

Nieris' detections can't sense her. He doesn't know she's here.

He only looked at Kadka from the side of his eye so Nieris wouldn't notice, but he waggled the fingers of his left hand to show he'd seen her. She pointed at the window, gave an exaggerated shrug.

She can't get in without drawing attention to herself. And if she could, there are wards. And if there weren't, Nieris could shield himself, or... There were a dozen different problems to deal with before she could get to him, and none of them were particularly easy to fix while he was stuck to the wall.

But Kadka had come when he'd thought no one could. And if he didn't do something, they were both going to die.

Calm down, Carver. Work this through. The flaw in the mage is the flaw in the magic. What's Nieris' flaw?

That was easy: arrogance.

He thinks he's the greatest mage alive. How does that affect his spells? He takes pride in the craft—he'll have chosen his wording carefully. But... how many is he keeping up right now? The wards, the binding spell, the detection spell on the bridge, the

Astral mask that blocked Indree's sending... and the portal. The most unstable and difficult of spells. More than any mage would risk.

Except maybe one who thought himself a true master.

That's where he's vulnerable. He's concentrating on too much at once. If I can distract him badly enough, he might drop something. It won't be the portal, and it won't be the binding—he won't risk letting me free. But if he doesn't think anyone else is capable of getting on board, he has no reason to hold his ward.

But Kadka still had to get inside. Just breaking the spells would make little difference if Nieris could simply cast them again. Breaking a window or opening the door would draw attention, and that would give the chancellor more than enough time to stop her with a spell—based on the efficiency of his binding, Tane had little doubt that the man knew his combat magic.

There wasn't much time left. The portal was large enough now to fit a man, a silver-blue hole in reality that only had to be anchored in place.

Kadka was still watching; Tane flicked his fingers at her, gesturing her away from the window, and she ducked aside. He tested the freedom of his wrists, gripped the pistol in his pocket, found the clasp on the charmglobe in the other.

He had a plan.

It wasn't easy with his limited range of motion, but Tane fumbled the pistol from his pocket, and aimed from the hip at Nieris. No shot would fly straight while the chancellor was channelling so much Astral power, but that wasn't the point. Unable to speak, Tane slammed the heel of his foot against the wall for attention.

Nieris halted his chanting with a frown, holding his nearly-complete portal in stasis, and glanced sidelong at Tane. His eyes fell on the pistol.

Tane pulled the trigger, and the firing charm consumed itself in a silver flash.

At the same time, Nieris shouted in the *lingua*, and a

shield of shimmering silver burst to life around him. The ancryst ball had already banked away from the strength of his magic, shattering through the window at the far left of the bridge. The pane of glass fell from its frame in great shards, and the roar of passing wind filled the room.

And for just a moment, Tane felt his bonds loosen as the shield drew some of Nieris' concentration. The ancryst would never have struck true, but throwing up a shield under threat was instinctive for any combat-trained mage. Which was exactly what he'd been counting on.

Nieris looked to the shattered window, and back to Tane. "Mister Carver, if you insist on interrupting, I will have to punish you." He glared at Tane, and his eyes glazed.

Pain lanced through Tane's temples like a white-hot spike driven directly through his brain. It spread over his body, a thousand hot needles stabbed directly into every nerve. He screamed silently into his magical muzzle, writhed against his bonds.

But he didn't let it stop him. Forcing his fingers open through spasms of agony, Tane rolled the charmglobe along the floor.

Nieris' eyes widened as he recognized the brass ball for what it was. He uttered a spell, sealing the charmglobe in a dome of magical force, and threw an arm across his face to shield his eyes against the possibility of a flash charm.

Another spell cast, and again, the energy holding Tane faltered. The muzzle on his jaw faded away, and the pain dulled. His arms were still bound, but it didn't matter. It was working.

The charmglobe clicked open inside Nieris' seal.

Nothing happened. It was empty.

The chancellor uncovered his eyes at the sound, and scowled at the empty brass ball. "I am losing my patience, Mister Carver!" he snapped. Again, that distant look in his eye.

The pain returned, worse than before. It seared through Tane's bones, boiled the blood in his veins, filled his skull until it felt like it would burst. He screamed, aloud this time, as every muscle in his body tensed and strained under the assault. He squeezed his eyes shut.

And in his clenched fist, he crushed the seal on the flash charm he'd palmed.

A burst of blinding light filled the room, bright enough to blaze red even through the flesh of Tane's eyelids. Nieris cried out in surprise. The pain abated, and Tane sagged several inches from the wall in his bonds.

He opened his eyes. The portal was still there, a door-sized oval of silver-blue, but the shield around Nieris was gone, and the one around the charmglobe. Which meant the spells Tane couldn't see might have failed too.

If they hadn't, it was over. He didn't have any tricks left.

Nieris clutched a hand to his eyes, his face twisted with rage. "Enough!" he bellowed, all illusion of gentility long since vanished. "You will not distract me with these petty—"

A blur of grey skin and wild white hair struck the chancellor hard in the side, tackling him to the floor. The portal flared wide and blinked out of existence. At the same moment, Tane's bonds failed. He collapsed to the floor on his knees.

"What about her?" he said, and lifted his head to look at Kadka.

She'd pushed Nieris up against the wall, pinning him there. The chancellor started to chant, but she clapped a hand over his mouth, and her knife was at his throat in an instant. "Say magic words and you die."

Tane pushed himself to his feet. His head throbbed with residual agony, and he was unsteady on the shifting airship floor, but he made it to Kadka. "You came," he said. "I didn't think anyone would."

She glanced at him, frowning. "Would be easier, if you don't leave me behind."

"I know. I'm sorry. I thought… I suppose I thought I could do it alone. I was wrong."

"Never again." A hint of that familiar grin, a flash of sharp teeth at one side of her mouth. "Or maybe I don't save you next time."

"Never again," he agreed.

Above, a great wail and moan came from the envelope. *Ah, yes. Imminent death.* Tane had absolutely no interest in falling from the sky aboard a broken ancryst vehicle—even his worst nightmares weren't as bad as that. There had to be some way to stop it.

He gestured at Nieris. "Uncover his mouth, but be ready if he tries anything. We need answers and we don't have much time."

Kadka leaned close to Nieris' face. "Remember. Faster to cut throat than say spell." Raw disgust and terror warred in the chancellor's eyes, but he nodded his head slightly. She removed her hand.

As soon as she did, Nieris spoke. "Call off your beast, Mister Carver. We can still be civilized about this. None of us want to die here. I can portal all of us to safety before the envelope breaks. All I ask is that you let me go."

"Let you go?" Tane felt his fist close, and before he knew what he was doing, he was swinging it at Nieris' jaw. His knuckles jarred painfully against bone, and pain shot up his arm; he'd never hit someone like that before.

Kadka gave him an impressed grin as he rubbed his hand. "Not bad, Carver."

Nieris spat blood from his mouth, and glared at Tane. "Are you quite satisfied? We haven't time to—"

"Shut up," Tane said flatly. "You do *not* go free, and this airship isn't going to hurt anyone. You killed my friend, and I'm not letting you turn the last project she worked on into your weapon. Or your symbol. You can tell me how to fix it, or you can die with us."

Nieris stared at him for a long moment, and then, "You believe that would be the end of this, don't you? If you save the airship and turn me over to the bluecaps." He laughed, sharp and bitter. "You truly don't understand what you've stumbled upon. The Knights of the Emperor are so much larger than one man. There are others, so many others, and they know that the time has come. They will carry on the work. If I… if I must die for the cause, so be it."

Knights of the Emperor? Tane didn't like the sound of that, but there wasn't time to worry about it now. "If you're so willing to die, why try to bargain to begin with? Come on, Nieris, you can still—"

Another moan from above, and then a loud snap. The airship listed sharply to one side.

Tane felt himself start to slide as the floor tipped upward, and then faster, and then he was hurtling toward the broken window. Lady Abena's unconscious body struck the wall before he did, and she was low enough that it stopped her.

Tane wasn't so lucky. The lip of the window took him in the thigh and swept his legs out beneath him. He tumbled out into the darkness, and his watch case slipped free of his pocket, swinging from his waistcoat at the end of its brass chain. Below, only the deck rail stood between him and an impossible drop to the city lights below.

His vision spun wildly as he fell. He couldn't tell which way was up—the night-time lights of the city below looked very much like the stars above. Too disoriented to grab hold, he struck the railing with his shoulder and bounced over. The impact spun him around so that he was looking back in the direction he'd come from. Just above the bridge, a section of the rigging that bound the envelope to the hull flapped free—it must have snapped as the envelope expanded. With one hand, Tane grasped wildly for the rail as he plummeted away from the ship.

He missed.

Suddenly Kadka was there, holding the railing with one hand. Her fingers closed tight around his wrist.

Tane dangled wide-eyed, too terrified to speak or breathe for fear that the slightest movement might shake him free of her grip. The ship adjusted to the sudden shift and righted itself as well as it could, though the hull still swayed and the nearer side of the deck hung considerably lower than the farther. Kadka found her footing, let go of the rail, and reached for Tane's arm with her now-free hand.

"Such an unfortunate turn." Nieris' voice, wretchedly smug. He appeared out of the dark behind Kadka, looming above her as she bent over the rail. "You did come very close to stopping me, I must admit." He started to chant a spell.

Kadka lashed her free hand behind her, but Nieris simply stepped out of reach. There was nothing she could do without letting Tane fall, and Tane was utterly helpless, hanging in the night sky. *He's won.*

Behind Nieris, the light shining from the bridge windows flickered and dimmed. The chancellor's mouth gaped open. His eyes rolled back in his head.

Glowing faintly against the night, a ghostly silver-blue hand thrust directly through his chest.

CHAPTER TWENTY-ONE

———

KADKA HEAVED TANE to safety as Nieris collapsed to
the deck. The wraith bent over the chancellor, feasting
hungrily. Still reeling, Tane could only watch, clinging to
the rail to hold himself upright.

Nieris' pale elven skin went paler still, and his veins
bulged out like dark worms burrowing beneath. He twitched
and spasmed as the wraith siphoned away his Astral bond,
but its grip was in him too deep now to pull away.

"Carver," Kadka said, gripping Tane's shoulder. "The
Lady Protector. Come."

Tane shook his head to clear it, and they skirted
around the feeding wraith toward the hatch that led back
into the bridge.

It was dim inside—the wraith had drained most of
the lights. Lady Abena lay unmoving against the left wall.

Kadka bent down beside the Lady Protector, and held
a hand just above her nose and mouth. "Still breathing,"
she said, and looked up at Tane. "What now? We have to
stop this, yes?"

"I... I don't know how. We need to stop the power
going to the heating glyphs to save the envelope, but if we
pull the gems, the lift spells lose power too, and the whole

ship will fall out of the sky. If we even make it that long."
Tane jabbed a finger toward the broken window, where the
ghostly figure was still siphoning power from the chancellor.
"That thing is distracted for now, but Nieris won't last
forever." Absently, he grabbed the watch case dangling
from his waistcoat and clutched it tight. "Astra, I can't see
any way out. I'm sorry I pulled you into this, Kadka."

She shook her head. "No. I make you let me come,
remember?"

"At the beginning. But you came *here* to help me."

"Some. Also I want to ride airship." She grinned.
"But I can't let friend fight insane mage alone. My choice,
not yours."

"Well I'm sorry anyway. For all the times you've
saved me, I don't think I've been a very good friend in
return. Not good enough to deserve this."

She shrugged. "In Sverna, everyone looks at me like
human. Here, everyone sees orc. You look at me like
Kadka, even if you are stupid sometimes. Show me magic
like I have never seen. Is enough." With one white-furred
hand, she clasped his shoulder. "If I die flying on airship
like no one ever has... is not such a bad death. But if
anyone can stop it, I think you can. Fighting is done,
Carver. Time for cleverness now."

He wanted more than anything to tell her he had
something. Some solution to justify her faith. But he
didn't. He had nothing. "Kadka, I—"

A long screech cut him off, and the airship lurched
again, this time directly downward.

The deck fell under their feet, and Tane's stomach
rose into his throat. He lifted into the air as if he was
entirely weightless; beside him Kadka did the same, and
the limp figure of the Lady Protector.

And then, just as suddenly, the ship caught itself, and
he slammed down painfully on his hands and knees.

Kadka landed improbably on her feet, and caught Lady
Abena before she struck the floor. "What is this, Carver?"

"The envelope wasn't made to expand this much," said Tane, rising shakily to his feet. "One of the compartments must be losing air. The lift spells on the hull are trying to compensate, but with so much power going to the heating glyphs, they're failing. We don't have long left." He glanced out the window.

The sudden fall hadn't thrown Nieris overboard, but he'd been tossed limply against the railing. The wraith, unaffected by the movements of the ship, drifted easily back down to the deck. But it wasn't moving toward Nieris anymore. It was coming for the bridge. For them. *And this time I don't have an engine case to trap it… wait.*

He grabbed Kadka's arm and jabbed a finger toward the instruments at the front of the bridge. "Take the wheel. Steer us out over the water if you can. If this works, it might be a rough landing. If it doesn't, we can still save the people below us."

The wraith passed through the window as if it wasn't there and drifted toward the nearest source of Astral energy: Lady Abena, in Kadka's arms.

Tane stepped around them to block the way.

"This way, you ugly wisp of mist." He didn't think the weak insult would do much to draw its attention, but saying it made him feel a little bit more confident.

The wraith turned lightning-blue eyes toward him, and reached out a hand. Tane leapt back, but not far enough to lose its attention. And just as he'd hoped, it followed, closing the space with increasing speed now that it had chosen its prey. With Nieris gone, Tane's was the strongest Astral signature in the room—unconscious, Lady Abena's would be relatively dormant.

Kadka hadn't gone for the wheel yet. Instead, she lowered Lady Abena to the floor and took a step toward Tane. "Carver, what—"

He waved her off, backing rapidly away from the wraith as it closed on him. "Just take the wheel! It doesn't want you, and we have to get it away from the instruments.

Trust me, Kadka. I'm doing something clever." *I hope*. The door to the lower decks was just behind him now, and he stepped backward over the threshold. "Come on, fog-face. Follow me!"

It did, blurring toward him with unnerving speed.

Tane turned and ran.

———

Kadka tied off the ropes, lashing Lady Abena's unconscious body to the wall beside Chancellor Nieris—she'd dragged him in from the deck, in case they still needed him. He was conscious, but he didn't resist, just stared blankly and went where he was led. There were cords and fastenings all around the bridge; whatever they were supposed to be used for, they worked well enough for this. She couldn't look after the Lady Protector and do what she had to do at the same time. It was safer this way.

She strode to the wheel, took it in both hands, turned it just a bit to the right. There was resistance, but it moved slightly. A moment later, the airship began to turn. Kadka grinned. She didn't know if she'd get out of this alive, didn't know what Carver was doing, or even if *he* knew what he was doing. But for a moment, she didn't care.

She was *flying*.

The lights of the city spun slowly, far below, as she maneuvered the ship's nose toward the Audish Channel. There it was, coming into view through the right window pane, a dark expanse against a coast speckled with light.

They were still too high. If the ship fell from this height, it wouldn't matter if they were over water or earth. Kadka glanced at the instrument panel; there were two large wood-handled levers, one on either side of the wheel. Each was currently set at a different angle, with space to move forward or back. She had no idea what either of them did, but if one didn't control descent, this airship had been built very stupidly.

Guessing at random, she grabbed the one on the right, and pushed.

The ship lunged ahead at speed. Kadka gripped the wheel to keep from stumbling back under the sudden acceleration, and her weight pushed it further right. Suddenly the airship was turning too hard and too fast.

"*Deshka!*" She pulled the lever back down, and the ship began to slow. Grabbing the wheel in both hands once more, she levelled out the turn as gently as she could.

It had to be the other one, then. She took the left-hand lever and pushed it forward, slow and gradual. At first, it seemed as if nothing had happened, but after a moment, the coastline started to rise over the nose of the ship. With a satisfied nod, Kadka steered in the direction of the bay.

A deafening screech from overhead, and the airship dropped again.

Kadka's feet lifted off the floor; she gripped the wheel tight to keep from being slammed against the ceiling. Against the wall, the ropes held Lady Abena and Nieris in place. The abrupt descent only jostled them slightly.

Once more, something arrested the fall—the lift spells, Carver had said—and Kadka slammed back to the deck, barely keeping her legs under her.

They'd dropped further this time. And they were still high enough that if the spells on the ship couldn't stop the next fall, everyone on board would be thoroughly crushed on impact.

It was up to Carver now. Whatever plan he had, she hoped it worked, because she didn't think they had long left.

———

Tane sprinted down the stairs from the bridge, and then along the hall toward the rear of the ship. He didn't know the layout, but it wasn't hard to guess the direction

he needed to go. The floor trembled and moved underfoot, but he didn't have time for vertigo. Steel hatches
flashed by on either side; he ignored them. Walls and
doors wouldn't stop the wraith. His shadow on the walls
shifted as lights flickered and died behind.

It was getting closer.

Pressure filled his ears, and then a voice. Ree. "*Tane!
You're alive! I couldn't reach you!*"

"*Nieris had a mask up. But I have bigger problems now.*"

Ahead, at the far end of the hall, he saw what he'd
been hoping to see: a hatch, similar to the others, but
made of brass. That had to be it. He glanced over his
shoulder—the wraith was no more than a few yards
behind him, a silver-blue phantom with arms outstretched.
Lightning-blue eyes fixed on Tane, unblinking.

He put his head down and ran with everything he
had.

"*Tane, what are you—*"

All at once, the floor leapt under his feet. The ship
accelerated, turning hard to the right, and he was thrown
against the wall. "*Spellfire! Keep it steady, Kadka!*"

He didn't realize he'd sent the words to Indree, but
she answered. "*Is she steering the ship? It's turning back toward
the coast.*"

He didn't have time to send back. The wraith closed
the distance as Tane tried to get his balance again. A
ghostly hand reached for his chest. He threw himself back,
and silver-blue fingers passed through the air inches short
of contact. Tane grabbed the railing and launched himself
forward once more into a stumbling run.

He reached the hatch, gripped the wheel, pulled it
hard. It turned, but too slowly. Again, he looked back—
the wraith was nearly on him. He wasn't going to make it.

The wraith reached out. There was nowhere left to run.

The ship lurched downward into sudden freefall.

Tane held the hatch wheel as his body lifted into the
air. The wraith, unanchored, rose sharply through the

ceiling to the upper level.

It lasted longer than the first time, but just as Tane was certain he was plummeting to his death, the lift spells re-engaged and caught the ship. His weight returned, pulling him back to the deck.

The wraith was still somewhere above, but it could pass through the deck like air. It would be coming back. Tane wrenched hard at the brass wheel.

"*Tane?*"

"*Indree, I don't know if I'm going to get out of this alive.*" The wheel moved easier the further it turned. He spun it until he felt the latch give way, and pulled the door open. The room beyond was fully lined with brass, insulated against outside magic. "*If I don't see you again… I'm sorry. For everything.*"

A ghostly silver-blue figure descended through the ceiling above, just a few feet behind him.

"*Tane, I don't—*"

Tane stepped through the door, and the pressure in his ears died, blocked by brass. Indree was gone.

But he'd made it. The engine room. Against the back wall, a glass-fronted hatch held an array of a half-dozen fist-sized diamonds. The first two were already entirely lost to milky white, cracked and lustreless, and the next two were heavily clouded over from the unchecked drain of the heating glyphs. The last pair, though, was still clear enough that Tane could see the brass of the wall behind them. All were grasped in claws of conductive copper, and all along the walls, brass tubes—no doubt lined on the inside with copper as well—ran from the sides of the power array to the left and right sides of the room. On both sides, large panels allowed access to the inner workings of the ancryst engines.

There was no way out. If this didn't work, he'd trapped himself with the wraith at a dead end.

Tane ignored the engines, and lunged for the hatch at the back wall. With both hands, he yanked it open. Even without looking, he could *feel* the wraith behind him, reaching. He ducked, threw himself to the right, scrambled away. Braced himself for that cold spectral touch.

It didn't come.

He turned to see the wraith's hands thrust into the power array.

Yes! The only source of Astral energy on the ship that had a chance of distracting a wraith from living prey was the gem array that powered the spells keeping them in the air. Tane hadn't been sure they'd have enough charge left, but it had worked.

He leapt through the door, slammed it shut behind him, turned the wheel hard. The latch clicked into place.

The wraith was trapped, sealed in brass.

Trapped with the ship's power source. Which didn't give them much time.

Tane sprinted back down the hall, up the stairs, through the door to the bridge. It was dark inside—the last of the magelights had given out.

"Kadka!" She was at the wheel, a silhouette against the starlit sky. He closed the distance to her side. "How long before we can land? We don't have much time." Against the left wall, he noticed Lady Abena and Nieris lashed tight beside one another. Good—he didn't much care about the chancellor, but the sudden drop before might well have dashed the Lady Protector against the roof.

Kadka glanced at him as he drew alongside her. "Don't know. Hard to tell, like this." She gestured at the windows. The lightless expanse of the bay was beneath them now, just like Indree had said, but it was difficult to judge their height in the dark. "What did you do? Where is wraith?"

"Locked in the engine room, siphoning the ship's gems. Which should drain the flow to the heating glyphs before the envelope bursts. Whatever air is left, it will help to slow our fall when the lift spells end. But it's not going to keep us aloft. If we're too high when the power runs out…"

He met her eyes, and saw that he didn't have to finish. She nodded her understanding, and smiled slightly, without showing her teeth.

"Is good we meet each other, Tane Carver. Has been… exciting." She offered him her hand.

Tane took it. He didn't know what else to say—or maybe there was nothing *left* to say. Hand in hand and side by side, they waited silently as the ship descended over dark waters.

It wasn't long before the lift spells failed.

CHAPTER TWENTY-TWO

─────

THERE WAS NOTHING else for Tane to grab, so he grabbed Kadka, throwing his arms around her. She gripped him tight with one hand, holding the wheel with the other as they rose into the air together.

Nothing stopped them, this time. The power was spent. For what felt like forever, they plummeted toward a black sea.

And then, with a great splash, the airship hit water.

Through the window, the dark of the bay surged outward in a massive wave, just visible in the reflected moonlight. He and Kadka hit the floor with jarring force, still clinging to one another. Kadka landed atop him, crushing the breath from his lungs.

But they weren't dead.

Thank the Astra! Whether they'd been nearer to the water than he'd thought or sufficiently slowed by what was left of the envelope, he didn't know, and it didn't matter now. All that mattered was that he was still alive.

Alive enough to feel the full weight of Kadka's knee digging into his ribs.

"Get off," he wheezed. "Can't breathe."

She rolled off of him on to her back, laughing. "That

was... not so bad."

"Speak for yourself," Tane groaned, clutching his side.

Across the room, Lady Abena stirred against the ropes holding her. "What... what happened? Nieris!" She glanced to her side, saw the chancellor lashed beside her, and tried to recoil. Nieris only stared at her, his mouth gaping open. A string of drool fell from his lower lip.

"He's harmless, Your Ladyship," Tane said. "Kadka, let her free." Painfully, he started to rise as Kadka bounded up and drew her knife. She'd freed Lady Abena before Tane had gotten himself to his feet.

Lady Abena let Kadka help her up and leaned against her, blinking in confusion. "You... how did you do this, Mister Carver? Last I remember, you were in no position to stop Talain."

He glanced at Kadka, and smiled. "I didn't do it alone. But it's a long story." A light drew his attention. More than one, actually, visible through the bridge windows. Boats, moving over the water. "And it looks like help is coming. We wouldn't be very good hosts if we didn't greet them at the door."

The three of them made their way down to the side hatch, and Tane threw it open. The boats were only a few yards out now. There were two of them, cutters powered by ancryst engines, both dwarfed by the airship. In the silver-blue of their magelights he could see the constabulary's golden shield on their prows, marking them as coastal patrol vessels.

"Tane?" Indree's voice.

"I'm here," he said. "We're alive."

The first boat raised a ramp to the hatch, and three human Mageblades were the first ones off the deck. One took Lady Abena from Kadka while the others fell in protectively on either side. Tane moved to follow as they took her back down the ramp, but one of them raised a hand to stop him.

"The next boat is yours. The Lady Protector's security can't be compromised."

Tane didn't argue, although it was tempting. *Where
was that security a half-hour ago?*

From the deck, Lady Abena turned back one last
time. "Thank you, Mister Carver, Miss Kadka. I will not
forget this." And then her Mageblades led her into the
cabin, and out of sight.

The next boat had barely raised its ramp before a figure was marching toward them, flanked by several
bluecaps in full uniform.

"Not the most elegant landing," said Indree. Up
close, he could see that her evening dress was soaking wet.
The wave they'd raised when they hit water must have
thrown up a powerful spray.

"Sorry," Kadka said, grinning. "But is not bad for my
first time, I think."

"No," said Indree. "Not bad at all." She turned to
Tane, then, and before he knew what was happening, she
had her arms around him. "I'm glad you're alive."

Instinctively, Tane folded his hands around her
waist. "I'm glad you're glad," he said. "I... thought you'd
be angrier."

She drew back, but didn't let go. "Oh, I'm *very* angry."
She smiled to take the bite from the words, but he could
see the annoyance behind her eyes. "You nearly got yourself shot, and it wasn't exactly easy to explain why I
stopped the Mageblades from killing a man chasing after the
Lady Protector with a stolen pistol. But you did it. Somehow. So this time, I'm going to skip the scolding."

Kadka leaned close to Tane's ear, and *far* too loudly,
she whispered, "Now you kiss."

He should have been embarrassed, but it was just too
absurd, after everything. Instead, he quirked an eyebrow at
Indree. "I do hate to disappoint an audience..."

Indree hesitated, just an instant, and then shook her
head and pushed him away. "In your dreams. I have work

to do. Where's Nieris?"

Tane pointed back through the hatch. "Tied up on the bridge. He won't give you any trouble. He's been Astra-riven."

"What?" Indree frowned. "How did a *wraith* get on board?"

"I'll tell you later," Tane said. "When you're done working. It's trapped in the engine room. You'll need to have someone banish it."

Indree took a pair of bluecaps in with her, and directed one—a gnomish man she introduced as Constable Tobtock—to bring Tane and Kadka aboard the smaller boat. He led them down the ramp and into the ship's cabin. There wasn't much to it, just a small enclosed space with a bench along one side and a small cot bolted to the floor.

"Sit where you like," Tobtock said. "It will take some time to properly secure the airship. Can I get you something to drink?"

"Whiskey," Kadka said quickly, before Tane could answer.

Tobtock smiled. "I probably shouldn't, but after the night you've had… I might be able to find something. Wait here." He stepped out of the cabin and left them alone.

Tane sat down on the edge of the cot. Kadka lowered herself onto the bench and leaned against the wall. For a long time, they were both quiet, and then their eyes met across the room. That sharp-toothed grin spread across Kadka's face, and Tane couldn't help but match it.

And then they were both laughing, letting the tension spill out of them in the only way that seemed to make sense just then. Just like in the workshop, the day they'd met.

It was a long time before they stopped.

CHAPTER TWENTY-THREE

———

"NO ONE WORKED harder on the airship project than Allaea did. I always admired that about her, even while I was trying to get her to rest for a night or two."

Indree stood behind a podium atop a dais erected on the grass at the campus center, before an audience of hundreds of students and citizens. She wore her full constable's uniform, with her cap held at her side. Her voice—magically projected to reach the furthest corners of the crowd—rang in Tane's ears as if he was standing right beside her, though he was actually sitting beside Kadka several rows back.

"She loved her work. She loved the University. But she was just as dedicated to her friends. Since we were children, she would drop everything to help me when I really needed her. She could be blunt, and sometimes it hurt to hear, but her advice always went straight to the heart of the problem. I wouldn't be who I am today without her." Indree stopped, there, and wiped a hand across her cheek. Tane couldn't see the tears, but he knew they were there.

"But even though she's gone, she'll be remembered. By the friends whose lives she touched, and by her family"—

there, she gestured at Allaea's parents, an elven couple sitting on the dais behind her—"and by everyone who looks up to see an airship passing by overhead. Soon that will be a common sight, all across Audland and the Continent. She would say that she was only responsible for a small part of it, that there were hundreds of others who worked on the project. And as usual, she would be right. But even if it's only in part, our nation owes its mark on the sky to her."

Indree looked up, then, at the clear blue afternoon sky. "Thank you, Allaea. You won't be forgotten." And then she stepped away from the podium, and returned to her seat beside Allaea's parents and the University deans. The Hesliars stood to embrace her.

Lady Abena rose next, and stepped up to speak. "Thank you for the beautiful words, Constable Inspector Lovial. Miss Hesliar was truly one of the University's best. And in honor of her great contribution to the project, I am proud to announce that a name has been chosen for our first airship: the Hesliar."

Cheers from the crowd, and applause like thunder. Allaea had been well known on campus, and well liked, despite her sharp tongue. Tane stood with a hundred others to clap for the friend he'd lost, and Kadka did the same beside him.

Lady Abena held up a hand as the applause died. "Now, there is one more announcement to make. As some of you know, with the airship project completed, Chancellor Nieris has decided to take his retirement after more than a century of service."

A few sounds of surprise, there.

"Should say he is drooling in his bed," Kadka grumbled. "Is criminal and murderer. Should tell truth."

"You know they can't, Kadka," Tane said quietly. "I don't love it, but if the full extent of what happened got out, the Continent would never trust our airships, and the treaty would fall apart. Lady Abena was lucky she was able to pass off last night as a final test flight." The full blame for Allaea's murder had been laid on Randolf Cranst. Who *had* been the one to actually kill her, but still, it felt like a lie. It wasn't as if Nieris had gotten off easily, though—everything the man was had been stripped away, including the magic he'd been so proud of. He'd spend the rest of his life an Astra-riven invalid, being cared for by his family at some estate in the countryside. House Nieris had been as eager as anyone to keep his crimes quiet.

"As Protector of the Realm," Lady Abena continued, "it falls to me to select a worthy individual to fill the rather large shoes Talain Nieris leaves behind. As such, it is my pleasure to present to you your new chancellor: Liana Greymond."

That wasn't entirely a surprise. There hadn't been a non-elven chancellor for a very long time, but there were no elven deans to raise up, and Dean Greymond was a well-respected mage. Tane applauded again as Greymond took the podium from the Lady Protector.

"Thank you, everyone," Greymond said. "I will strive to live up to the legacy of my predecessors. And as my first act, Lady Abena has graciously given me permission to announce a new program, in honor of the many non-magical laborers and mechanical engineers who worked on the airship project."

Tane couldn't help but rise a little bit in his seat. *She can't mean...*

"Beginning with the next term, we will be opening the University's schools of magic to the non-magical. All who pass the entrance exams will be welcome. The Protectorate's great strength is our magic, and the Lady Protector and I agree that all of our citizens deserve the opportunity to understand and work with it, whether they are born with magecraft or not."

As the crowd gasped and shouted and cheered, Tane's hand found his father's watch case. He held it tight as tears rolled down his cheeks. After all this time, all the years he'd worked for this, he couldn't believe it.

Kadka was looking at him. He swallowed, embarrassed, and moved to wipe his cheeks. But she only put a hand on his shoulder.

"No shame, Carver. Is dream long time coming. Enjoy it."

So he did, until the noise of the crowd began to fade. It was only then that he found himself wondering, *What am I supposed to do with myself now?*

Greymond dismissed the crowd, and the seats emptied quickly as people stood and filed down the aisles. But Tane didn't move, just sat where he was for a long time, gathering himself.

Kadka waited patiently beside him until she couldn't anymore, and then she nudged him and pointed to the dais. "Come, or we miss them. You can talk to Indree." She waggled her eyebrows suggestively, and then started across the grass, not waiting to see if he was behind her.

Indree was still with Allaea's parents, exchanging goodbyes, but Lady Abena and Dean Greymond—*Chancellor* Greymond, Tane reminded himself—were already climbing down the steps. Tane followed Kadka over to catch them before they left.

"Mister Carver, Miss Kadka," Lady Abena greeted them. "I'm pleased you accepted the invitation. After hearing the story you told the constables, I may never be able to repay you. I wish that we could have given you the recognition you deserve. If there was any way to do it without revealing how close the airship came to disaster…" She looked to Tane. "But Liana suggested that you might appreciate the validation of your thesis as some degree of compensation."

"It's more than enough," said Tane, and looked to Greymond. "Thank you."

"You earned it," Greymond said. "I wouldn't have thought even a trained mage could best Nieris, but you stopped him without any magic of your own. I was wrong about you, Tane, and you've more than proved it. If you'd

like, we'll need lecturers who understand the viewpoint of
our non-magical students. There could be a position for you
here."

It was more than he'd ever expected. He didn't have
an answer ready; the words came out in an embarrassing
stammer. "I… I'm not sure I'd know how to…"

"You don't have to decide now," said Greymond.
"Just think about it." And then, to Kadka, "And Miss
Kadka, needless to say, there is a position in the University
Guard for you if you want it. We owe you just as much as
Mister Carver."

"I will think too," Kadka said. "Is good that you offer. Maybe you are better to work for than Nieris."

Greymond arched an eyebrow, and smiled slightly. "I
hope I am, Miss Kadka. I truly do."

"Now," said Lady Abena," we must be going. There
is a great deal of work to do getting the University and my
airships back in working order. Come, Liana."

"What about—" Kadka began.

Greymond, predictably, was already answering. "Ah,
yes. I nearly forgot. I've arranged for the bursar to release
your pay. You can see him on your way off campus." With
that, she and Lady Abena departed toward Thelan's Hall,
surrounded by an escort of a half-dozen Mageblades.

Indree approached then, holding her cap under her
arm. "Tane. Kadka. I'm glad you came." Her eyes were
tired and sad, rimmed with red, but she offered them a
shallow smile.

"Is good speech you give," said Kadka.

"It was." The corner of Tane's mouth quirked upward. "Allaea would have hated it."

Indree laughed, and it brought a hint of brightness to
her eyes. "She would have, wouldn't she? But I think she
would want me to thank you. Both of you. Without your
help, her killers would never have been brought to justice."

"There might still be others, if what Nieris said about
the Knights of the Emperor was more than just an empty

threat," said Tane. "Have you found anything on them?"

"Not yet. I think that might be a more long-term investigation. But we have Cranst's badge, and we'll be going through Nieris' home and office over the next few days. Speaking of which, Tane... if we *do* find something, I might be able to offer you some consulting work. We don't know how many of these people there are, or how high they go. If they exist, we're going to need help finding them. And you've proven to be good at that."

"I'll help however I can."

"Good," said Indree. She paused for a long moment, as if unsure what else to say. "Well. I should get back to the Yard. There's work to be done, like I said."

"Right," said Tane. Another pause, broken by Kadka faking the most unsubtle cough he'd ever heard and prodding him sharply in the ribs. *Spellfire, she's going to make me do it.* "Er, Indree... maybe you'd like to get dinner, some time? And talk about... things?"

"I think I might like that," Indree said, with a slow smile. "I'll let you know." She turned to go, and then looked back at him over her shoulder. "And Tane? You can call me Ree."

————

An unmarked envelope was waiting in Tane's letter-box when he and Kadka arrived back at his office. He sat behind his desk to examine it, and Kadka took the seat on the other side, putting up her legs.

"What is it?" she asked.

Tane broke the seal and pulled out a small sheet of folded paper. At the top, it was marked with the image of a green masquerade mask. "I think it's from Bastian." He read it aloud. "My friends. On behalf of all the Audish patriots who will never know the great service you have done our nation, let me thank you. Consider yourselves welcome guests in my establishment, and know that you will always merit a generous discount. Signed, an ardent admirer." He smiled as he read the next bit. "Postscript: My dear Kadka, the offer always stands. If you are ever in need of work, please present yourself to our mutual friend the fishmonger."

Kadka laughed. "Is him. No question."

"So," said Tane, "are you going to take him up on it? For a criminal, he seems like a good sort. And it might be exciting. I know you like that. Or are you going back to the University Guard?" Part of him dreaded her answer. Now that it was all over, he knew she'd have to find some sort of reliable work, but discussing it aloud felt more final than he liked.

"Don't know yet," Kadka said. She hesitated, and then, "You have choice too. Teach at University, work with bluecaps. What will you do?

"I suppose I'll lecture," he said, without much enthusiasm. "The pay is going to be better than anything I've made working on my own." It was strange—he'd spent ten years of his life worrying about proving his worth to the University, and now that he'd done it, the prospect of returning was less exciting than he'd imagined. Indree had already forged her own path, and Allaea was gone. After all this time, it didn't feel like there was anything left for him there. "Or... maybe the bluecaps would be better. Maybe both, if the timing works. It's... more options than I've had for a long time."

Kadka nodded, and after a moment, she said, "Feels strange, not to work together. Is not many days since we meet, but... seems longer."

"I know," said Tane. "But this case was an anomaly. I've been calling myself a 'consultant' for years now, and even split between us I made more coin today than I have over the last two months. There isn't enough work for—"

A knock at the door interrupted him. He shared a glance with Kadka—he wasn't expecting anyone, but if Nieris could be believed, there might be other Knights of the Emperor, and they might know who he was. They both stood; her hand went to her hip, where he knew she had a knife hidden.

Tane made sure the door-chain was fastened tight, and Kadka put her back to the wall, knife in hand. Another shared glance, and at her nod, he opened the door a crack to peek through.

There was no one in sight.

"Hello," a voice said at waist-height. He looked down to see a matronly gnomish woman with dark hair standing just outside the threshold. "My name is Telna Dookle. Are you the ones they're calling the Magebreakers?"

Tane blinked. "I don't... what? What in the Astra is a Magebreaker?"

"The ones who stopped Chancellor Nieris," she said, looking up at him hopefully.

"I think you're mistaken," said Tane. "The chancellor retired—"

"I know, I know." She wrung her hands, a worried frown on her face. "But I've heard another story too. There are rumors, people who saw things last night, and I hoped... They say you can help people without magic deal with magical problems?"

Tane closed the door just enough to slip the chain free, and then swung it fully open. If he was any judge of liars, this woman wasn't one. He beckoned to Kadka, and she moved into sight beside him. "I'm Tane Carver, and this is Kadka. Exactly what kind of help are you looking for?"

"It's my husband," she answered. "About a week ago, he met an unlicensed mage at a tavern who offered to hire him for some sort of job. I didn't like the sound of it, but my husband—Tonke is his name—has always been stubborn. He wanted to give our family the things we couldn't afford, artifacts to make our lives easier. He engineers tunnels for the mines south of the city, and this man wanted his skills for... I don't know what. They were supposed to meet two days ago, and he hasn't come back!"

She wrung her hands again, tears building in her eyes. "I can't go asking after a dangerous mage by myself, but if I tell the constables, they'll ask what my husband is involved in. I'm sure it's nothing legal. If they lock him up at Stooketon Yard... we have *children*, Mister Carver. They need their father. Can you help me?"

Tane looked down at Telna Dookle for a moment, and then his eyes met Kadka's over the little woman's head.

A sharp-toothed grin stretched across Kadka's face. "Seems like job for Magebreakers."

"I suppose it does," said Tane, and found himself smiling back. "Although I can't say I love that name."

Mrs. Dookle's eyes widened. "Does that mean you'll help me?"

Tane stepped aside, and ushered her toward his desk. "Mrs. Dookle, you came to the right place."

ABOUT THE AUTHOR

———

Ben S. Dobson is a Canadian fantasy author. When he isn't writing to indulge his lifelong passion for epic tales, he can probably be found playing Dungeons and Dragons, or watching a Joss Whedon show, or something equally geeky.

If you're interested in being notified when I release a new novel, sign up for my mailing list on my website, or at this address:

http://eepurl.com/g9dzw

For more information, check one of these places:
Website

http://bensdobson.com

Facebook

http://www.facebook.com/bensdobson

Email

bensdobson@gmail.com

Made in United States
Troutdale, OR
08/17/2024

22091690R00137